Jess Vallance

TO BE
PERFECTLY
HONEST

HOT
KEY
BOOKS

First published in Great Britain in 2019 by
HOT KEY BOOKS
80–81 Wimpole St, London W1G 9RE
www.hotkeybooks.com

A CIP catalogue record for this book is available from the British Library.

ISBN: 9781471407673
also available as an ebook

1

This book is typeset using Atomik ePublisher
Printed and bound in Great Britain by Clays Ltd, Elcograf S.p.A.

Hot Key Books is an imprint of Bonnier Zaffre Ltd,
part of Bonnier Books UK
www.bonnierbooks.co.uk

Also By Jess Vallance

Featuring Gracie Dart:
You Only Live Once

The Yellow Room
Birdy

TO BE
PERFECTLY
HONEST

PART 1:

Where we are all living a lie

The Idea of a Party

It was Friday night and I was on my way to a party. This was not a normal Friday night for me.

It wasn't just any party either. It was a warehouse party, on an industrial estate, where an actual DJ would be playing music on actual decks. I was excited by the way it all sounded. It sounded fun and cool and a little bit crazy.

In fact, I was so excited by the idea of the party that I was forcing myself to ignore the part of my brain telling me that the reality might not be quite as good.

I had been to parties before, but I wasn't yet convinced they were for me. I'd heard about good ones happening, but the ones I found myself at always seemed to just be people I didn't know very well sitting around in cramped rooms, talking about nothing and drinking out of plastic cups. And that was basically what we did every day in the canteen anyway. Except, at least in the canteen you could buy chips and we all had our own chair to sit on.

Everyone else was very excited about the location, but I think maybe the industrial estate element was putting me off. Industrial estates were cold and dirty, weren't they? Full of dark shadows and big signs for companies you'd never heard of. They were the kind of place you go with your dad on a Saturday morning to wait in the car in the rain while he talks to a man in overalls about how many bags of cement it takes to make a driveway.

Still, none of this mattered because even if the plan had been to hold the party in a toilet-brush factory, there was still no way I would be missing it. I was only in my second week at Coniston College, for heaven's sake. If I started being the kind of person to turn down party invites in favour of staying at home to watch *Gardener's World* with my parents at this delicate stage in my life, I might never shake the label. I might never get invited anywhere again.

I was with Til, my oldest friend, and Reeta, my newest. Til and I had been friends since we were thirteen. Reeta I'd met just two weeks earlier, in my psychology class. The three of us had gathered on the corner at the bottom of the hill outside Til's block of flats, as arranged, to walk up to the party together. Til was wearing what she always wore – black jeans, black boots and a black jumper. Reeta, for some reason, was wearing a rainbow tutu and pink fairy wings.

'It's not fancy dress, is it?' I asked, suddenly alarmed. I hated fancy dress but I hated the idea of being the odd one out more.

'No,' Reeta said, twirling around on the pavement like a ballerina. 'I just like to wear a statement piece.'

Til raised an eyebrow. 'What statement are you making? That you're insane?'

'Til!' I said. I was used to Til's bluntness but I thought it might be a bit early in the friendship to be unleashing it on Reeta like this.

Reeta seemed unfazed though. She just grinned, shrugged, took out a four-pack of Snickers from her bag and ate one in two mouthfuls. Reeta was always eating but her four-times-a-week cross-country running hobby meant that she was still no wider than a lamp-post.

'Energy,' she explained. 'For the rave.'

She offered me one, but I shook my head. I didn't want to turn up at my first industrial warehouse party smelling of peanuts.

'Where are we going then?' I asked Til.

'It's up the hill,' she said. 'Round the corner.' She made a vague swooshing movement with her hand.

'How far is it?' Reeta asked, adjusting her wings as if she might be contemplating flying there.

'Twenty minutes,' Til said. 'Ish.'

Til's idea of twenty minutes, it turned out, was actually nearer fifty, and it was almost completely dark by the time we arrived at the tall wire fence holding a plastic sign saying:

COLDTREE INDUSTRIAL ESTATE

In the four corners of the car park, there were floodlights on poles but they didn't throw out much light. With the tall buildings casting long shadows and the drizzle that had started to fall, the whole place felt more like the set of a Sunday night Victorian murder programme than the

9

scene of a lively social gathering.

Reeta shivered and looked around her. 'Doesn't feel much like a party.'

Til shrugged. 'That's 'cause we're stood in the car park, innit. We're not there yet.'

'So where do we have to go?' Reeta asked.

Til peered at her phone, using her hand to shield the screen from the drizzle. 'It's Unit 2B.'

The host of the party was a boy from college called Archie Dunbar and the music was to be provided by his brother, Lewis, who was a real-life DJ in a real-life club. (On Wednesdays he was, anyway. On the other days he made sandwiches at Subway.) The invite to the party had gone round college like a Mexican wave. You'd hear rumours of it from afar – where it would be and when, stories of how good Archie's parties had been in the past – so by the time someone officially associated with it wandered over and said, 'You should come, if you like. Friday night,' it was hard to stop yourself from kissing them on both cheeks in delight.

'Where is everyone?' Reeta said, pulling her coat on over her front, like a dentist putting on a plastic apron, so as not to interfere with her fairy wings. 'Shouldn't there be people around?'

'We're probably just really early,' I said. 'Or else they're all inside.'

'But inside *where*?' Reeta said.

'Listen.' Til stopped suddenly and we all stood still, our eyes narrowed as we tried to hear past the sound of the rain, which was getting steadily heavier. 'Hear that?'

There was a rhythmic *thump* coming from the other side of the car park – the sound of three bassy beats and then a higher crunching sound, in a repetitive pattern.

'Is that the decks?' Reeta asked, wide-eyed. 'Is that what decks sound like?'

Til shrugged. 'It's obviously what these ones sound like.' She pushed her hands into her jacket pockets and strode off towards the sound. Reeta and I followed.

'Yeah, this seems right,' she said as we approached a three-storey building with a corrugated roof. She looked down at her phone and then up at the building again. 'Archie said the warehouse was above a bathroom shop or something . . . and look.' She nodded up towards a sign. Big blue plastic letters spelt out:

WASH STOP

'Sounds like a bathroom shop, right?'

I shrugged.

The music was louder now we were right outside. I could feel it vibrating up my legs.

'I can see people!' Reeta said, excitedly pointing up towards a second-floor window.

As we looked up at the window, a light came on and went off again. Then a figure walked past, then another.

'But how do we get in?' I pulled on the metal door handle but it was locked. 'Are we just supposed to go through the shop or what?'

'Archie said he might need to let us in,' Til said. 'Call him.'

11

I did as I was told.

Archie took forever to answer the phone. 'You're there already?' he said. 'Bit keen, aren't you?'

I felt my cheeks get warm. No one had told us a specific time. How was one supposed to be fashionably late to a party when no one was very clear about exactly what time was unfashionably early?

'Uh, yeah,' I mumbled. 'We were on our way back from a . . . thing, so we thought we might as well just come now and . . .'

Archie sighed. 'Lewis is in there now getting set up, but he won't want anyone up there yet. You can wait downstairs though. He usually sets up like a chill-out area for when it gets a bit much for people, with drinks and snacks and stuff.'

I listened to Archie's directions to this so-called chill-out area, all the time trying not to feel too alarmed by the idea that the party might be the type to get 'a bit much'.

So-Called Chill-Out Area

We headed around the side of the building as Archie had instructed, and after a bit of scrabbling around in the dark, we managed to find the door he'd mentioned. We let ourselves in.

We looked around us. After a few moments, Til said, 'Well, this is OK then. Inside, at least.'

'Yeah,' I agreed. 'It's good to ease in gently, isn't it. Don't want to walk right into a rave off the street.'

The truth was, I was a little disappointed by the chill-out area. I'd had visions of bean bags, fairy lights and wind-chimes. Maybe bubbles floating around gently in front of us from some unseen machine and snacks served on silver trays. But actually the room wasn't even really a room – it was more of a corridor, with a row of wooden benches along one wall and lockers along the other. But then who was I to say what a chill-out area should look like?

We sat in silence for a minute, looking around us. The bassy rhythmic music was still going on above us.

'That's what's good about chill-out rooms,' I said, as if

I had seen many in my time. 'You can still hear the tunes, but you can talk too.'

I saw Til's eyebrow twitch a little. I think it was because I said 'tunes'. It had surprised me too, to be honest.

'It's kind of mesmerising,' I said. 'When you let the rhythm in, it really gets to you.'

Reeta nodded her head in agreement. Or in time with the music. I wasn't quite sure.

Another fifteen minutes went by. 'How long do you think we have to wait?' Reeta said. 'How long does the chill-out bit usually last?'

Neither Til nor I replied. Having already been made to feel quite silly about being so keen and early, I didn't fancy calling Archie back to ask. We'd just have to wait till things got going. I hoped it would be worth it.

'I'm so *hungry*,' Reeta said, her most common announcement. 'I thought Archie said there'd be drinks and snacks in this chill-out area? I can't see any snacks.'

'There's the machine.' Til nodded over to the vending machine, partially stocked with Cokes, Kit-Kats and Wotsits.

'And look,' I said, standing up and going over to a small table at the end of a row of lockers, where there was a bowl of some kind of crispy snack. 'There are snacks here. I mean, you're not exactly going to get little vol-au-vents and mini burgers – it's not a wedding! It's an industrial warehouse dance party!'

I passed the bowl to Reeta. She peered at the crispy balls closely, then took a handful and put them in her mouth. She chewed with her head on one side. 'My dad does mountain climbing,' she said, 'and when he's on a trek he has these little packets of cakes that taste a bit funny but they're specially designed to release energy slowly and make your body absolutely ready for climbing. Do you think these are like this?' She looked at me hopefully. 'Do you think at an industrial warehouse dance party they put on special snacks to help you party all night?'

'Probably,' I said. I was starting to feel fairly sure that I wasn't up to partying for even one eighth of the night.

Reeta kept eating until the bowl was almost empty, and we all carried on listening to the thumpy music, and I did actually start to feel quite chilled out in the chill-out area. That was until the door opened, a man in overalls stepped into the room and I sat up straight in alarm.

'Can I help you?' he asked, drying his hands on what looked like a grubby old T-shirt.

'Uh . . .' I looked at him. He looked too old to be at college. In his thirties, at least. But then Archie's brother was older, and who knew how many people had been invited to this enormous wild party. I really didn't think he was dressed for a party though. He looked a bit sweaty and dusty.

'We're here for the party . . .' I said. I felt silly for some reason, saying it out loud. 'The party thing, I mean. The warehouse thing . . .'

He frowned. 'You what?'

Til had been lying across the full length of a bench, but she sat up now. 'Is Archie here?' she said. 'Do you know when we can go up?'

The man looked blank and shook his head. 'Archie? No. Nah. Just me and Kev tonight.'

I didn't know this man or 'Kev' but a party with just two people didn't sound like much of a party at all. And where was Lewis, with the decks?

My phone rang and Til picked it up from where I'd left it at the end of the bench. 'Well, we're in the chill-out area, like you told us. Where are you?' She sounded impatient. 'Yeah, we're literally –' She stopped talking suddenly, and turned to me. 'What's the name of this bathroom shop?' She tried to crane her neck to see the sign that was directly above us. 'Wash something?'

'Wash Stop,' the overalls man said, throwing his T-shirt-slash-hand towel over his shoulder. 'It ain't a bathroom shop though.'

'What?' I said.

'Wash Stop,' Til said into her phone.

'It's not a shop at all,' overalls man said.

Til looked at him. 'Huh?'

'Wash Stop doesn't sell anything.'

'What is it then?' Reeta asked.

He shrugged. 'Industrial launderette, innit.'

We looked at each other.

'Archie, is it an industrial launderette, this place?' Til said into the phone. Then she turned back to overalls man. 'So just to confirm, this building isn't Waterworld, a luxury bathroom design company with a basic but spacious warehouse on the floor above it? A warehouse currently being set up for an all-night dance party?'

'You what?' Overalls man frowned and shook his head. He was getting annoyed now, I could tell. 'I've really got no idea what you're on about, but you kids can't be in here. It's a private building. There's machinery here.'

'Archie definitely said it was a bathroom shop,' Til said, looking at the man out of the corner of her eye like he wasn't quite to be trusted.

'Yeah. Waterworld *is* a bathroom shop, ' he said. 'But this ain't Waterworld. This is Wash Stop, the second largest industrial launderette in England. Waterworld – and its no doubt lovely warehouse – is at Birchwood Park.'

'Birchwood Park is miles away!' I said.

He nodded. 'Four or five.'

'If this isn't Waterworld and if Lewis isn't up there sorting out the massive party tunes on his decks, how come we can hear the music?' Reeta said, standing up and putting her hands on her hips. 'How come we can *hear* the massive party tunes? That music can't be coming from four or five miles away.'

The man pulled a face. 'That's not music. That's the machines.'

'Machines?' I asked quietly.

'Washing machines. Twenty-five commercial-sized washing machines, working their way through two hundred and thirty-six duvet covers, right at this moment.'

Til and I looked at each other, and then down at the floor.

'But –' Reeta began, but I put my hand on her arm to silence her.

I'd realised what had happened and I didn't want the man to have to spell it out. What had happened was that for the last forty-five minutes the three of us had been nodding along, appreciating the sweet melody of twenty-five industrial washing machines in operation.

A cat came through the door, and wound itself round the leg of a bench.

'A cat!' Reeta said, her confusion about the music immediately eclipsed. She crouched down on the floor to greet it.

'Rocky,' overalls man said. 'Office cat . . . probably wondering why you're eating his food.' He nodded towards the nearly empty bowl of snacks next to Reeta. She looked down at the bowl, then at the cat, then back to the bowl again. 'Cat . . . food . . . ?'

The man grinned and shrugged. 'I prefer a Kit-Kat and a cup of tea myself, but each to their own.'

Reeta stood up very slowly, took three deep breaths, then ran outside and vomited vigorously into a bush.

Theoretical Party Animals

Overalls man, whose name turned out to be Alan, had fetched us a bottle of water and a towelling cloth to help us look after Reeta. He'd actually been very considerate, given that we were technically trespassers. And cat-food thieves.

After nearly an hour walking in the rain, another hour sitting in a corridor listening to the sound of industrial washing machines and thirty minutes holding back Reeta's hair while she sicked up a stomach full of cat treats into the undergrowth, when we discovered there wasn't going to be a taxi free to take us the five miles across town to where the actual party was, I was more relieved than disappointed, although I didn't let on.

'Ah well,' I said with a shrug. 'I guess we'll just have to go to the next one.'

'Gutting though,' Til said.

'Yep,' I agreed with a sad sigh. 'Still, at least they knew we were up for coming in theory. It was just the execution of the plan that let us down.'

'Yeah,' said Til.

'Totally,' said Reeta. 'We're still totally party animals. In theory.'

Til's mum was on a late shift so the three of us headed back to hers to spend what was left of our Friday night watching telly.

Once we were inside and I had changed into a pair of Til's pyjama bottoms, Reeta flicked through the channels, eventually choosing us a programme called *Britain's Best Scarecrows*.

Now the whole pitiful launderette episode was over, it actually started to seem quite funny.

'I didn't want to say anything but I did think it looked weird, as soon as we went in,' I said, laughing. 'I mean, what kind of chill-out area has wooden benches and no windows?'

'Shut up you did not,' Til said. 'You were well into it.'

'I wasn't!' I said. 'You were the one who seemed to think it was all completely normal. I don't even know what a chill-out area is! I was just following your lead!'

'How the hell was I supposed to know what it was meant to be like?' Til said. 'I don't think it's even an official thing. I think Archie made up the whole idea of a chill-out area. Anyway, you were the one dancing to the sound of the washing machine.' Til put her hand up to her ear like she was listening to an invisible ear piece and nodded her head as if entranced. 'You were like "nice tunes, man!"'

I couldn't help but smile. 'I maintain that those washing machines had an irresistible beat. They want to think about selling a sample to some record producers or something.'

Reeta shook her head and stared off into the middle of the

room. 'I can't believe you gave me cat food to eat though, Grace. I may never get over the trauma.'

'You're the one that ate it!' I said, throwing an empty raisin box at her head. 'Don't blame me, you nearly cleared the bowl. It must have tasted OK!'

Reeta frowned. 'It tasted weird. Like really fishy and *weird*. But I thought that's just what snacks are like in chill-out rooms! I thought it was just because they were high energy. I didn't know what was going on at all but you two seemed to think it was all normal.'

'You know,' I said, stretching out on the sofa and putting my feet on the arm, 'I'm not sure parties in warehouses on industrial estates are for me. Right now, I can't think of anywhere I'd less like to be.'

'Me neither,' Reeta said, crinkling her nose in disgust. 'I think big parties are gross.'

Til and I both looked at her. 'I thought you were properly up for it,' Til said.

Reeta shook her head. 'Nope. You seemed to think it sounded cool and I didn't want to be a big old boring Norman staying in on my own.'

'Well, it wasn't exactly my first choice of a way to spend an evening,' Til said, throwing a piece of popcorn into the air and catching it in her mouth.

I sat up and folded my arms. 'This gets better and better, doesn't it? We've just spent half our evening totally and shamefully failing to get into a party we were all only pretending to want to go to in the first place. We are losers with a capital *loo*.'

In Your Shirt and Tie

The Monday after our Friday evening in a launderette corridor
was exactly like every other weekday morning in my house.

There were five of us in our family, so five people all
needing to get from unconscious to presentable in the space
of one hour. As usual my older brother, Ollie, nineteen,
couldn't find at least half the things he needed to survive
the day – his phone, his keys, his lunchbox, his jeans. And
as usual my little brother, Paddy, three, had come up with a
strange requirement that had to be fulfilled before he would
let Mum take him to nursery. On this particular day, he had
decided he wasn't a human, but a car (specifically, a Renault
Clio) and that like any car, he needed to be filled with petrol
to fuel his movement. This meant I had to spend a full three
of my precious getting-ready minutes holding the garden hose
to his ear and making a noise like a chugging petrol pump
before he would put on his shoes and plod out to the car.

When Mum and Paddy were safely on their way, Dad and I
waited in the car for Ollie so Dad could drop us at college on
the way to whichever work it was he was doing that day. Dad

had two jobs: something to do with training and computers for the railway, which he hated but paid the bills, and two days a week the job he didn't hate, being an instructor at the water sports centre at the marina. Monday was a computer-job day, so that meant he was wearing a suit and a tie and a miserable face.

So far, so normal for a Monday.

But then some things happened that weren't normal for a Monday.

Number one was that both my psychology lesson and my tutor meeting were cancelled. That meant that Til and I had a completely free afternoon. It had been raining all day, my shoes had got wet and my jeans were so tight and uncomfortable I swear they were giving me actual bruises, so Til and I decided to come back to my house at lunchtime to make toasties and watch telly.

I was expecting to get home to an empty house, so when I opened the front door and heard voices in the kitchen, I assumed Ollie must have come home, probably with a mate. But then Til and I went in and I was surprised to find not just Ollie, but Mum and Dad too, all sitting around the table, eating crumpets.

Dad stood up suddenly, wiping his mouth with a tissue. 'What are you doing home?'

If he hadn't done that, if he hadn't sprung up guiltily like I'd caught him snacking on a live mouse, I wouldn't have thought too much of it. It was unusual for everyone to come home for lunch, but not unheard of. But the way they were all looking at each other, then back at me, and the way Dad seemed to be in a hurry to put his tie on, I felt nervous.

'What are *you* doing home?' I said. 'Why are you all here?'

Mum stood up and went over to the sink and busied herself washing the plates. 'Just popped home for lunch,' she said.

This made me even more suspicious. For one thing, Mum always turns her back to me when she's lying and she gets a strange, high-pitched tone to her voice that I think she thinks is 'breezy'. For another thing, she was washing the plates by hand when we had a dishwasher. It seemed clear to me this was specifically so she could turn her back to me, specifically so she could lie to me.

I looked at Ollie. He was looking intently at his phone, but I could see there was nothing at all on the screen – so he was just avoiding making eye contact with me too.

'What's going on?' I demanded.

'Nothing!' Dad said. 'I've got to get back to work.'

He stood up and adjusted his tie in the reflection of the oven door. Ollie was looking at him strangely. Then Mum went over to him and put her hand on his arm.

'Come on, love,' she said. 'This is silly. It isn't going to work in the long run, and it isn't necessary.'

Dad's shoulders sagged and he sat down in his chair. 'Well, it isn't now, is it? It's not going to work now you've said *that*.'

'What?' I said again. 'What isn't going to work?'

There was a silence, then Ollie said, 'Dad lost his job.'

Dad scowled. 'Oliver!'

'What?' Ollie looked annoyed. 'Like Mum said, it was never going to work. She's not an idiot.'

'Who's not an idiot?' I said. 'Me? Which job? Lost how?'

Dad just rubbed his face with his hand.

'The railway,' Mum said.

'Oh,' I said. 'Well . . . that's OK? Isn't it? You didn't like that one anyway?'

'It was the one that paid the real money though,' Ollie said quietly.

I looked at Dad. Dad looked at Mum. They didn't argue with this.

'But it's nothing to worry about,' Dad said. 'We've got plenty to tide us over. The money Nan left us, for one thing. Everything's going to be fine.'

'When did it happen?' I said. 'This morning?'

Mum shook her head. 'A couple of weeks ago.'

I frowned. 'So where have you been going? In your shirt and tie? For the last two weeks?'

Dad sighed. 'Recruitment agencies. An interview, once. Or just . . . the library . . .'

Til looked at us all, her head on one side. She took a nectarine from the fruit bowl and started to eat it.

'You've been . . . pretending to go to work?' I said.

Dad shrugged.

'Told you it was crazy,' Ollie said, putting half a crumpet in his mouth in one go.

'And everyone knew apart from . . . me?' I said. I could feel my face getting hot.

'Well, Paddy doesn't know . . .' Mum said.

'Paddy!' I shouted. 'Paddy is a baby! Paddy doesn't know how many toes he's got!

'We just didn't want you to worry,' Mum said in a quiet voice.

'Great,' I said. 'Well, thanks for your consideration. And for treating me like a child!'

I left the kitchen, slamming the door shut behind me.

Til opened it again and followed me upstairs.

There are No Claws

In my bedroom, I think Til was trying to distract me because she started going into great detail about some argument she'd had with her plumbing tutor.

'He is obsessed with our cloths being clean. Like, holding them up to examine them for smudges. And I'm like, I'm not being funny, right, but we're standing in basically a toilet with filthy scum water up to our knees. Get over it, man.'

I turned the sound off the TV and turned to look at her. 'I just can't believe for over a week, he's been putting on work clothes and going out to "work" and then coming home and telling us about "work" and there was no work. *No work!* It's lying. I cannot believe the barefaced lying.'

'Yeah, I guess,' Til said with shrug.

'No guessing needed. It is a *fact*.'

Til shrugged. 'Maybe. But everyone lies. All the time. Everyone.'

'I don't,' I said.

Til laughed. 'Dude, literally the first conversation we had was a lie.'

'Was it?' I frowned, trying to remember.

'You told me you'd seen *The Exorcist* and you were so full of it that I said I'd seen it too. We had a whole conversation about the monster with the claws made out of screwdrivers. It was only two years later when I actually saw the stupid film that I realised you'd been totally making it up. There are no claws in *The Exorcist*.'

'Well, how should I know?' I said grumpily as I flicked through the TV channels. 'I've never seen it. Anyway, don't get all moral. You were lying too.'

Til nodded. 'Yep. Exactly my point. We're all at it.'

Ollie appeared in my bedroom doorway.

'Go away,' I said without looking at him. 'Co-conspirator. Enabler. Accomplice.'

He ignored me and came to sit on the end of my bed, peeling a satsuma and chucking the bits of peel across my room in the vague direction of the bin.

'When I was in Year Eleven, this really hot girl – excuse me, *woman* – asked me for directions when I was on the way to school. I managed to give her the directions no problem, even threw her a bit of the old Ollie-D charm and she was well into it, I could tell. Only thing was, I'd found myself doing the whole conversation in a kind of . . . Scouse accent. I don't know where it came from, but once you've committed to something like that you can't go back. Anyway, we say our goodbyes and that's that. Just a bit of early-morning flirting, I think to myself. But then I get to school, and Mrs Rogers says she wants to introduce us to the new student teacher. And who is she? She's Miss Hot Directions Woman, is who she is. I mean, what could I do? I did contemplate just talking in a Scouse accent for the rest of my life, but there was no way my mates were going to let me get away with that. I had to just pretend we'd never met.'

Til was laughing and I allowed myself a small smirk despite my displeasure.

'It's not really the same though, is it?' I argued. 'The same as outright lying to your own daughter's – your own sister's – face about something as important as having a job or not having a job.'

Til shrugged. 'I think you need to let it go. Lying is everywhere, right? It's like the . . . foundations of society. Look.' She picked up a magazine and flicked through a few pages. '"Make this delicious kale and fennel smoothie",' she read, and held up a photo of an unappetising beaker of swamp juice. 'Delicious? Lies. And this –' she pointed at a photo of a pot of face cream – '"Guaranteed to make you look ten years younger in two weeks". Ha! Gonna make me look like a six-year-old, is it? *Lies.*' She flicked through pages, jabbing her finger on photos and headlines. 'Politicians. Celebrities' "real" life stories. Lies, lies, lies. It's just how it works, Gracie. The world would fall apart if we all told the truth. Even for one day.'

'But how do you know?' I said. 'Maybe it wouldn't fall apart. Maybe it would be like drawing back a curtain, like sweeping away a cloud. Maybe if everyone was true and real and *honest*, the world would be transformed for the better.'

Til raised an eyebrow and looked back at her magazine.

'Like on Friday,' I went on. 'If you hadn't pretended that

that draughty corridor was exactly what you expected a chill-out room to look like –'

'Hey, you pretended too!' she said indignantly. 'You were the one getting down to the sound of the washing machine.'

'Exactly,' I said. 'We all lied because each other was lying and so we were just all going along with it like little sheep trapped in a cycle of our own lies. So much so that Reeta ate a bowl of cat food and was sick! What has life become that we'd rather eat a bowl of cat food than just be honest with our friends?'

Til didn't say anything. Ollie yawned and drifted off back to his room.

'I'm going to try it,' I said, sitting up and looking at Til. 'For one day. Surely it's possible for *one day*?'

'What is?'

'To not lie. Complete honesty. For one day.'

Bee on a Stick

The day I selected for my one-day trial of total honesty was the following Saturday, and on this particular Saturday we were having the big family lunch we always have one weekend in the middle of September because Mum, her sister Louise and her brother Jimmy all have their birthdays around then.

Mum's sister, my Auntie Louise, has two children – my cousins. Kai was ten and had a way of wearing his face in a little sneer that made it look like he was smelling something awful. Harriet was eighteen, although you wouldn't know it if you met her. She spoke very quietly, always seemed to be wearing horse riding clothes for no apparent reason and her only topic of conversation seemed to be schoolwork. She was, frankly, a bit boring.

Mum's brother, Uncle Jimmy, didn't have any children but was quite like a child himself. Every time we saw him he'd have a new idea that he was incredibly excited about and was sure was going to change the world. One year he was obsessed with a plan to cross-breed the chilli and the tomato to make an instant spicy tomato. Another year he came to us with a book full of sketches of something he was calling the 'Scat' – an all-in-one bobble hat and scarf. But after Mum pointed out that he'd basically reinvented the balaclava, he sat at the end of the table looking grumpy and saying no to more potatoes even though you could tell he wanted them.

This Saturday we had an extra guest – Auntie Louise's new boyfriend. Mum had given us all a briefing about how Louise was nervous to introduce him because she'd been single for so long, so we were all supposed to be especially friendly and welcoming. This got off to a slightly shaky start when Paddy ran up to him, put both hands on his (only very slightly round) belly and shouted, 'A BABY'S COMING OUT!'

Being totally honest before the guests arrived, when it was just Mum and Dad and my brothers at home, hadn't been too tricky. I'd told Paddy to get out of my room because he smelt like Marmite, which he did, but there was nothing new about that. I told Ollie I'd used his razor to shave my legs because I couldn't be bothered to buy my own and he'd barely even looked up to grunt his response. I told Mum I thought that yes, her dress was OK but I preferred the blue one with the stripes on the sleeve and, if anything, she seemed grateful for the fashion tip. It was almost too easy. I wanted the guests to hurry up and arrive so I could begin my experiment properly.

When I heard the doorbell, I looked out of my bedroom window and I saw Uncle Jimmy on the drive, wearing loose rainbow-coloured trousers and a tie-dye T-shirt. Jimmy's personal image changed as often (and with as much enthusiasm) as his ideas. This month it looked like he was trying to pass himself off as the kind of man who lived in a van and played bongos for a living, which I suppose is a better look than 'plastic cup salesman from Peterborough', which is what he actually was.

'Gracie!' he beamed when I came into the kitchen. Paddy was crouching on the floor hiding in the flapping fabric of his bright trousers. 'You look gorgeous, as ever,' he said.

This was a lie. But normally my impulse would have been to join in with the lie-fest with gusto: 'I've missed you! So good to see you! Sorry I didn't text you back the other day, my phone's playing up!' Nonsense, all of it.

'I don't think you really think that, but thank you for being nice,' I said. Then before he could protest, I added, 'You look very colourful. I don't often see so many different colours in one outfit.'

This was fine, I thought. No judgement, just a simple observation. And as luck would have it, Jimmy seemed to take it well.

'Aw, thanks!' he beamed. 'I've been reading a lot about the effect of colour on mood and I'm just trying to spread a little joy!'

I just smiled and nodded.

'Hey, I got you something.' Jimmy grinned and put his tea on the side. 'A little present. For passing your exams in the summer.' He reached into his rucksack and pulled out a short bamboo stick with a small knitted bumble bee on the end.

'It's . . . a bee on a stick!' I said as I took it. This was true, after all.

The whole bee situation had got out of hand a long time ago, and had itself come about because of false enthusiasm – aka a *lie* – on my part.

When I was a few years younger, Jimmy had sent me a picture frame as a birthday present. Tasked by Mum to write him a thank-you card, and struggling to think of much to say to expand on the basic 'thanks for my present', I had resorted to commenting on the picture that had come with the frame – a bland piece of stock photography printed on flimsy paper showing a bee resting on a flower. Unsure how to sign off my gushing thank-you note, I'd ended up going with, 'I do so love bees.'

But Uncle Jimmy had taken that comment to heart, and now every gift I received had an apian theme. (Apian means 'related to bees', which I know because these are the things you talk about with your uncle who thinks you have a bee obsession.) T-shirts with bees on. Bee-shaped mugs. An A3 wall chart explaining the anatomy of a queen bee. One year he'd particularly excelled himself and bought me a bright yellow-and-black striped jacket that had a hood topped with bee antennae.

'Oh lovely.' Mum beamed encouragingly now. 'Isn't that kind? You love bees, don't you, Grace?'

I was annoyed that Mum had directly asked my opinion on the bee. If she hadn't, I could have left my reaction to the present as, 'It's a bee on a stick!' and 'Thanks!' and nothing untrue would need to have passed my lips. But

I could tell Mum thought this was funny. Uncle Jimmy and the bees had become a running joke in the family and I was tempted to confirm, for the eighth year running that, yes, I did indeed have an almost unhealthy preoccupation with bees.

But I stopped myself. When would this end, if the snowball of lies kept on rolling? Would I be standing at the altar on my wedding day wearing a bee mask? Would I be the only OAP in my retirement home with a bumble-bee duvet cover? I felt guilty, and a bit sad, that Jimmy was spending all this time carefully choosing these presents for me – and most of them ended up in charity shops. And I said I'd wanted to stop lying. A day of total honesty. That's what I'd signed up to.

What should I say though? What was the honest response to 'You love bees, don't you, Grace?'?

'You know,' I began, 'I don't have anything a*gainst* bees. I understand they have a very important role in the ecosystem –'

'Oh, totally,' Jimmy said enthusiastically, obviously thinking I was gearing up for another pollination chat (there had been lots of those over the years).

'But,' I carried on before he could say anything, 'I'm just not sure I'm quite as keen on them as I might have led you to believe. I'm just not quite sure that, at this time in my life, I have a pressing need for a knitted bee on a stick.'

Mum's face froze and she looked from me to Jimmy. Jimmy stared at me.

Then Mum opened her mouth to speak – to tell me off, or to apologise for me, probably – but before she could say anything, Jimmy started to laugh.

'Gracie, you've made my day!'

'Really?'

He nodded. 'Absolutely! I didn't know how much longer I was going to be able to go on for, every year, finding a new bee present. I just don't know if there are any more bee things in the world. I have, as you can probably tell, started to get a bit desperate.' He took the bee on a stick off me and waved it around in the air. 'Even when I bought it, I thought to myself, this has to be the worst gift ever. If that niece of mine likes this then she is surely not quite right in the head.'

I laughed. 'Oh, cheers.'

In the end, we passed the bee on a stick on to Paddy who spent a few joyful minutes waving it above his head, then thrusting it into each of our faces and shouting, 'Ribbet!'

That's All You Do

I felt energised by the success of my frank bee confession. It hadn't upset Jimmy. In fact, he'd seem pleased, and now he and I were laughing and joking in a more genuine way than we had for ages.

I found myself on a bit of a roll.

Over lunch, Jimmy made a jokey comment about being my favourite uncle. He didn't out and out ask me, but he said, 'But I am your favourite uncle, aren't I?'

I put my head on one side. 'Maybe second favourite.'

Jimmy laughed. 'Oh yeah, who's my competition?'

'Paul,' I said. 'He's a bit funnier than you, and you often tell the same story over and over. Which is OK, but I'm just never sure how to react – whether to pretend I haven't heard it before or not, you know?'

Jimmy started to laugh. And then so did Louise, and Mum and Dad.

'It's funny because it's true, Jim,' Louise said. 'I can't believe no one's told you before.'

* * *

After lunch, when the adults were all in the kitchen discussing the benefits of underfloor heating, Harriet and I sat awkwardly side by side on the sofa. After a few moments of uncomfortable silence, she said, 'So how is psychology A level going? How have you found research methods?'

'Yeah, OK,' I said, looking down at my hands.

We were quiet again. 'Which topics do you have on your syllabus?' she asked.

I could have listed the subjects, I suppose – that would have been an honest enough response to the question – but I was keen to push myself. Honesty didn't just mean true facts, I decided. It meant being genuine and sharing what was in my heart. And actually, I'd been dying to say this for years so it was quite convenient I had my one-day honesty spree as an excuse.

'The thing is, Harriet,' I said with a sigh, 'I get a bit bored talking about school and college work with you all the time. Isn't there anything better we can talk about?'

For a moment, Harriet looked like I'd slapped her. I thought she might even cry. But then she said, 'Really? But you *love* that stuff.'

'What stuff? Do I?'

Harriet nodded, her nose crinkled. 'Yeah! I mean, don't you? I got the impression that's all you do. School stuff, I mean. Coursework. Exams.'

'What? I do not. Not any more. Maybe there were a few months back there when I got bit . . . carried away. But not now. I did think that's all *you* do though. It's all you talk about anyway.'

Harriet frowned. 'Only because that's what I thought you wanted to talk about! I have to look it all up beforehand so I've got something to ask you. I even make notes – see?' She held out her hand and I could just about make out the words 'qualitative' and 'quantitative' written on the back of it.

I looked at her hand, my head on one side. 'What . . . ?' I started, bemused. 'But you . . .'

But in the end I just laughed. Laughed at the idea of poor old Harriet sitting down at her computer to do actual research and making notes just so she could get through a conversation with me.

'So what *do* you like?' I asked. 'I can't think of a single thing you've told me you do for fun since you were eleven and you turned up at lunch with that puppet theatre you'd made out of toilet rolls.'

'Oh yeah!' Harriet grinned. 'I was so proud of that!'

For the first time in nearly three years Harriet and I had a conversation that didn't involve us listing our subjects and grades, often with a slightly resentful, competitive undertone, and for the first time in three years, I realised that actually, Harriet was kind of all right.

Everyone came into the lounge for cups of tea and more talking about DIY and loft insulation and how often chimneys should be swept and I kept looking at my watch wondering how much longer it was all going to go on for. I guess I wasn't being as sly about it as I thought because after a while Auntie Louise said to me, 'Are we keeping you from something, Gracie?'

She said it with a grin and I opened my mouth to say 'Oh

no, not at all' automatically. But I stopped myself. Instead, I took a deep breath and told her the truth:

'Well, not right now, no. But the thing is, I did want to go to my friend's house tonight and if I'm going to do that I need to do some work for college first but I don't know if I'm going to have time to fit that in so I might have to stay home this evening instead to do it. So basically, if you're still here in forty-five minutes' time, then yes, the honest truth is you will be keeping me from something – keeping me from going to my friend's house.' Then I added, 'But it is lovely to see you all.'

'Grace!' Mum said sharply.

'You're on form today!' Jimmy said.

'Sorry,' I said with a shrug. 'I'm just being honest.' Then after a moment, I added, 'I think the problem is, we only ever talk about the start times of things, don't we? We always say "Come over about one!" but we never say "And then leave at three". It would make life easier if we did. Don't you think?'

They all just looked at me but then Louise said, 'She's right, you know. I've lost count of the times I've had to tell people I've just got to pick the kids up from swimming or that I've got an appointment with the accountant, when what I really want to say is "Time to go now! Things to do! Can't be sitting around with you all day!"' She chuckled and shook her head.

'Exactly!' I said. 'Exactly my point.'

Anyway, it worked because about twenty minutes later, they all left. And it was all fine. It wasn't awkward. No one seemed annoyed or like they were being thrown out the door. Everyone kissed and said goodbye nicely and I was free to get my work done, then head over to Til's for movies and pizza, just how I wanted.

This is a Hostage Situation

'You've been rather strange this afternoon,' Mum said to me as we cleared away the lunch things. 'Has someone done something to offend you? First all that business with Jim about the bee presents, then telling them all to leave. I was quite embarrassed, Grace!'

'Well, you shouldn't have been,' I said. 'I was just being honest. And that's supposed to be a good thing.'

Mum looked at me, frowning slightly as she scraped leftovers into the bin. 'Is this to do with Dad?' she asked.

I shrugged. 'Maybe. I just don't know why you lied. It makes no *sense*.'

'We explained all this,' Mum said. 'Sometimes we lie to protect people.'

'But maybe we don't need protecting!' I said. 'Jimmy didn't need protecting from the harsh truth that I'm just not that into bees. In fact, I probably caused him way more trouble by pretending to like them because now he's had to spend half his life searching for presents on bee-stuff-for-weirdos dot com! And I don't need protecting either. I'm much more upset about the lying than the fact Dad has to get a new job.'

Mum sighed. 'OK,' she said. 'Point taken. Sorry.'

'It's OK,' I said, taking glasses from the dishwasher and stacking them in the cupboard. 'At least I know everything now.'

But Mum didn't say anything. She turned away and started vigorously scrubbing melted cheese off a glass dish. I gave Ollie a questioning look, but he just looked down. Then he slunked out of the door.

I finished emptying the dishwasher then went upstairs. Ollie was in his bedroom, looking through a drawer.

'What's going on?' I said, standing in the doorway.

He jerked his head up. 'I'm looking for a T-shirt to wear out tonight. My Stone Roses one. Have you got it?'

'No,' I said. 'I mean with Mum and Dad. They're being weird. They're being all silent. They're still not telling me something, I'm sure of it. It's so obvious.'

'I dunno, do I?' he said, continuing to rummage. 'Nothing to do with me.'

I sighed. If my entire family wanted to get away with being such enormous liars, they needed to get better at it.

I looked around Ollie's room. Then I went over to his desk and picked up his deodorant.

'You're going on a date tonight, aren't you?' I said.

He made a face. 'Not like a *date* date. But she's going to be there, yeah.'

'Lily?'

He nodded. 'How do you know?'

'Marvin told me.'

Ollie rolled his eyes. Marvin was Ollie's best friend and he never stopped talking. I could find out more about Ollie from talking to Marvin for ten minutes than I could from asking a year's worth of questions to Ollie himself.

'Anyway,' I went on, still holding the deodorant, 'if you're going on a date, you're going to want to smell nice and fresh, right?' I bet Lily loves it when you smell of . . .' I turned the can around to look at the label. '. . . "fresh temptation"? Seriously, how is that a smell?'

Ollie smirked and made a lazy lunge for the can, but I easily held it out of his reach.

'And,' I said, picking up his bright-green hair gel, 'You're going to want to do your hair with that spiky front bit you like.'

Ollie narrowed his eyes.

'And that means . . .' I said slowly, '. . . that means, you're going to have to . . .' I turned and ran into my own bedroom, his deodorant in one hand, the hair gel in the other. I slammed the door shut and shouted through the gap. 'You're going to have to tell me what's going on! Otherwise the deodorant *and* the hair gel get it.'

I pushed my chair up against the handle so no matter how hard he rattled he wouldn't to be able to get in.

'Grace!' he said. 'I seriously haven't got time! I need to get ready. My hair's a mess.'

'Your hair looks fine,' I said. And then, because being honest means being honest even when it's not convenient, I added, 'In fact, I really like it since you had it cut. It looks much better.'

'Oh. You really think?' he said. I heard him take a couple of steps across the landing to look in the mirror. 'I was worried it was all a bit fluffy. Like a baby rabbit.'

'Just *tell* me, Ollie,' I said through the door. 'And then we can both be on our way.'

'There's nothing to tell,' he said, banging on the door again.

'Then I guess you'll be going out with baby rabbit hair,' I said, sitting down on the chair with my back to the door.

He was silent for a full minute and I was just contemplating the idea that maybe there really was nothing to tell, maybe I'd got the wrong end of the stick, when Ollie said, 'Fine. I'll tell you. But open the door.' He had his mouth pushed right against the crack and was talking quietly. He obviously didn't want Mum and Dad to hear he was about to give up their secrets just so he could look nice for a girl.

I opened the door. He held out his hand for his things, but I put them behind my back. 'You talk first,' I said. '*Then* you groom. Is it to do with Dad's job thing?'

Ollie nodded, and looked down sheepishly.

'What?' I said. 'What else is there?'

'They're skint. It's not true that they've got money to tide them over. Nan's money is gone.'

'How?'

'Dad invested it in the sailing school. They needed a new boat to keep it running. He says he'll make it back . . . but who knows when.'

'So what's going to happen?'

Ollie shrugged. 'I don't know. I guess they'll work it out, or they might have to sell the house.'

'Sell the house!'

Ollie shrugged again.

I wasn't sure what was worse – that I was about to be homeless, or that they'd lied about it.

Actually, yes I was. It was the lying.

Lying. *Again.*

PART 2:

Where I decide enough is enough

Sarah and My Official Proclamation

I had started seeing Sarah at the beginning of term, after an awkward summer of missed opportunities and misunderstandings.

I wasn't sure what 'seeing' each other really was. Neither of us had actually used the word 'girlfriend' but we did do a lot of kissing, which I thought I was getting quite good at. I wasn't sure we'd quite got the hang of conversation yet though. I think the problem was, the actual 'seeing' of each other didn't seem to be happening that often. I'd realised two things in the few weeks we'd been trying to get to know each other:

1) Sarah did a lot of stuff.
2) I didn't.

Sarah was in the year above me at college and planning to do medicine at university but it wasn't just her intense science A levels or her part-time job at the library that took up her time. She also had hobbies. 'Hobbies' wasn't really an idea I'd ever quite managed to get on board with. It seemed to me that rather a lot of hobbies were really just sports, and that was never something I was going to be interested in. But Sarah did lots of them, and that meant I had to fit in when she was free.

According to a brief text conversation we'd had in the week, Sunday evening was the next time Sarah would have a gap in her schedule, so the day after the honest family lunch, I headed to her house.

Sarah's dad let me in and I went up to her room. It was, as always, completely immaculate. If she wanted to read a book, she would take it down from the shelf, turn the pages carefully (never folding over the corners or anything untidy like that), then when she'd finished, she'd mark her place and put it back on the shelf, in the exact same spot. Everything had its place and she made sure everything was in it.

'Hey,' she said when I came in.

'Hey,' I said with a frown, which I realised I'd been wearing for the whole walk over.

'What's up?' she said, putting down her book.

I sat down on the end of her bed. 'My mum and dad is what's up. I'm angry.'

'Why?'

I told her about the Dad losing his job stuff, and about the money worries, and of the double-decker lie-upon-lying: first by pretending to be going to work and then, once they'd come clean and I'd made it quite clear how offended I was about being lied to, carrying on lying.

Sarah sat cross-legged and listened, her chin resting on her palm, a small crease between her eyebrows.

'The only reason I know now is because I dragged it out of Ollie,' I said at the end of my rant. 'So that's why. I'm angry about the lying.'

'Hmm,' Sarah said, lying back on her pillow with her hands behind her head. 'Maybe they thought it was for the best.'

'It wasn't,' I said, still scowling.

I looked at her, waiting for her to say something else, but she just reached for her phone. 'Hey, look at this – someone sent it to me yesterday.' She scrolled through and held it out to me.

I realised I was looking at a video of someone on a BMX bike. 'Is that you?' I said, not really caring either way.

Sarah laughed. 'No! It's Mark Unison, British Champion.'

'Right,' I said, passing the phone back to her without smiling, without actually watching the video to the end. I'd just told her about something that had been bothering me all weekend, big family stuff, and she'd just said 'hmm' and 'maybe' and shown me a video of a grown man playing on a tiny bicycle. I was annoyed. And Sarah could see it.

When I'd first met Sarah, at the library in town where I would often spend Saturday afternoons, I knew she rode a bike, but I'd always assumed this was just a way of getting about. What I hadn't realised was that, as well as her ordinary ride-along-the-road bike she had a BMX and BMXing was her main hobby.

She would head off to this park she always talked about, out on the edge of the Downs with all these others – boys mostly, in baggy jeans and little woolly hats – and ride her funny little bike up and down ramps and do hops and jumps and wheelies. I hadn't yet seen her in action in person but she'd shown me a wobbly video on her phone. I wasn't sure what I was supposed to make of it. It looked dangerous, for one thing. And for another thing . . . well, what was the point? It all seemed a bit unnecessary to me.

'Hey, come here,' she said. She pulled me down so I was lying next to her on her bed, my head next to hers on the pillow. She turned onto her side to look at me, her head propped up on her palm.

She touched my cheek, which made me feel a bit funny. She was very pretty, even when she was being monumentally unhelpful about my family problems.

'Don't worry about it,' she said. She said this a lot, and even though I knew sometimes she was right, it felt like what she was really saying was '*I'm* not worried about this'. And to me, that sounded a lot like she just didn't care.

I turned my head away from her and looked at the ceiling. 'Why does no one tell the truth any more? Does anyone even know how?'

Sarah laughed. 'I think you're being a bit dramatic, Gracie. It was just one thing. Your parents were just trying to do what they thought was right.'

She often called me dramatic, I'd noticed.

'It's not just that,' I said. 'It's everywhere. On the telly. Magazines. Even to each other. Friends, barefaced lying to each other, and everyone else is making out it's normal!'

I told her about my and Til's and Reeta's evening out in

the launderette corridor, listening to the sound of washing machines and eating cat food. And when she'd finished laughing about that, I picked up a magazine and showed her all the examples Til had pointed out to me the other day – celebrities peddling far-fetched promises about the benefits of their lifestyles, adverts making overblown claims, all of it.

'Is nothing *real* any more?' I finished, throwing the magazine down. 'Does anyone know what the truth even *is*?'

She laughed again, but I scowled, so she stopped.

'You're right,' she said in that calm, placid way she had. 'People lie a lot. But, I don't know.' She shrugged. 'That's just the way it is.' Then she went back to watching her BMX video.

'But . . .' I said after a moment. Then I stopped. I didn't know what I wanted to say. I didn't really know what my argument was. All I knew was that I wanted her to agree with me. I wanted her to agree that it was all annoying and I was right. I wanted to see her get angry about something. I wanted her to have an opinion. Any opinion.

'Well, I'm not doing it any more,' I said eventually, throwing the magazine onto the floor. 'I'm not accepting it. I won't go along with this ridiculous habit. I'm not lying ever again.'

It occurred to me then that maybe she was right – I was dramatic. But I couldn't help but feel this mainly came out when I was around her, when I was trying to get a reaction out of her. When I was trying to get her to be interested in me. So now here I was, exaggerating and making big promises, just to get her to take me seriously.

'Ever again?' she said, raising her eyebrows but not looking up from her video.

I thought about this. I'd liked having a one-day challenge. A definite timescale made it feel like a project and I'd always liked a project.

'OK maybe not *ever* again, but for . . . twenty days.' I paused. Was that ambitious enough? One day had been easy, after all. 'Actually, fifty!' I nodded to myself. 'Yes. Fifty days. That's a good number. A good, strong amount of time.' I stood up, ready to make my official proclamation. 'For fifty days, I will only speak the truth. Fifty days of total honesty.'

'OK,' Sarah said, scrolling through her phone to look for another video. 'Whatever you think.'

The Pledge

When I got home from Sarah's, I took an A3 sheet of yellow paper from the box on top of my wardrobe and in a black permanent marker I wrote:

The Honesty Policy

Then underneath, in smaller letters, I wrote:

(because, as they say, honesty is the <u>best</u> policy)

just for extra motivation.

Then I wrote:

For fifty days, I, Grace Georgina Dart, pledge to be completely, 100% honest at all times.

Next to this I did my formal signature – *Ms G. G. Dart* – just to make it clear I meant business.

Underneath my official declaration I drew out a table – five columns and ten rows – and numbered the squares one to fifty. Each square would represent a day, and only if I'd managed a day of complete honesty would I be able to cross one off. I found a ball of Blu-Tack under my bed, picked off the fluff, and stuck the sheet to the wall above my desk.

Then, because I felt like I needed a witness to hold me accountable, I took a photo of the poster on my phone and sent it to Til. A few minutes later, she replied.

Good luck with that.

Day One

The next day – Monday – marked day one of my honesty project. I'd woken up late and been in such a rush to get ready for college that I hadn't had time to say anything to anyone at home, honest or otherwise. By the time I got to college, I was so keen to put complete, one hundred per cent honesty into action that when I saw my psychology lecturer, Leroy, in the car park, rather than hurrying away to avoid polite conversation as I normally would have, I hung back so he could talk to me.

'Morning, Grace,' he said. I paused while he locked up his bike and we walked into college side by side. 'Good weekend? Get that brain poster done for me?'

He was talking about an assignment he'd set us the previous Thursday – to design a poster for a GP waiting room showing a diagram of the brain and explaining each of the main areas. I was pleased he'd asked. Here was something I was glad to be honest about.

'Sort of,' I said.

'Sort of?' He raised an eyebrow.

'Well, the thing was, I thought it was kind of a stupid task.' I felt a small rush of excitement. I would never have said that before. Here I was, embarking on my mission, saying exactly what I thought, regardless of the consequences. I pressed on. 'I mean, I can learn the areas of the brain just by reading that chapter in the book. And I've already done that; I do know the main ones. So I really didn't see the point in spending a whole afternoon trying to draw a lumpy old brain, and then sitting there for hours, colouring it in and making it look nice. What's the point? How is that going to help anyone? But then I also didn't want to just *not* do it because it's not really my style to be disobedient. Being a rebel scares me a bit. Plus, I know you were just trying to be an exciting teacher by giving us a creative task and I didn't want to be mean to you. So I did it. I did *do* the poster. But I just did it really quickly and it looks rubbish. Basically, I did the minimum I thought I could get away with without getting in trouble.'

'Oh. Right.' Leroy frowned slightly. 'I can see your line of reasoning, but you know, Grace, it has been proven that the best way to learn something –'

'. . . is to explain it to someone else. Yeah yeah yeah, I know, you've told us that like four times. But like I said, I have learnt it. I didn't need to do the poster.'

Leroy looked at me sideways. 'Hmm,' he said doubtfully. 'If you say so. I'll be testing you though!' And he strode off towards the staff area.

And that was that. A one hundred per cent honest conversation – with a lecturer, no less – and no real trouble. No drama.

I felt good. It was relaxing, actually, to just say exactly what was on my mind, not trying to guess what I was supposed to say, or what the other person wanted me to say.

I felt liberated.

Speed-Friending

On Monday mornings at college we had Tutor Hour, where we had to spend a whole period in our tutor groups while our tutor, Piers, talked about forms we had to fill in or gave us a little workshop on stress or finances or other things not directly related to our courses. In that Monday's session, Piers announced that we were going to 'try something a bit different' that day.

'I was talking to the other tutors,' he said, sitting on the edge of his desk, his feet resting on a chair, 'and we were noticing how there's a tendency with first years – with everyone, maybe – to really stick to your friendship groups quite tightly. Don't get me wrong, it's great to have a crew –' I saw Til roll her eyes at the word 'crew' – 'but it's a little early in the year for everyone to be so set in their ways. You all came from different places, different schools, different parts of the country in some cases, and we want to make sure that you've all had an opportunity to mingle, that you're not missing out on any opportunities to find a friend for life just because you don't study the same subject or because

60

you haven't been able to work up the courage to say hi to each other. So . . .' He stood up and pushed his hands into his pockets. 'What we're going to do is try a little . . . speed dating.'

There were a few sniggers and a lot of groans from the tutor group.

Piers laughed and held up his hand to quieten us. 'Not speed dating in the traditional sense. Not dating at all, really. We're not looking for romance – although of course what you do in your own time is up to you. We're just talking about making friends. Quick three-minute conversations to give you a chance to say hello and find out a bit about as many people as possible. Are we all up for it?' He looked at me for some reason. 'Grace, up for it?'

I nodded slowly. 'I'm willing to give it a go.' That was true enough. I felt I could say more though, in pursuit of real honesty, so I added: 'I think it might be awful but I've never tried it before and you seem quite pleased with yourself for thinking it up so I don't want to make you feel stupid by being grumpy about it.'

Piers laughed. 'Very generous.' Then he clapped his hands together. 'Come with me then, folks.'

With much scraping of chairs and rustling of coats the whole tutor group got up and followed Piers down the corridor and around the corner to the main assembly hall where there were already forty or fifty people from our year milling around by the stage. Thirty desks were set out in a horseshoe around the front of the hall with a chair on either side of each one, and a piece of paper in the middle.

'Right,' Piers said, taking a step up onto the stage. 'I'm going to give you all a number – one or two – then number ones take a seat on one side of a table. Twos, come and stand in the corner here, in an orderly queue.'

He rattled through the group quickly, assigning us all a number. I was a two, so I stood as instructed with the others while the ones made their way to a seat. Piers made us get in a queue and said that, on his whistle, we should sit down on an empty chair in the order we were standing.

'Stick to the order you're in please, folks!' he called. 'No skipping tables and choosing to visit your mates! That defies the point!'

'What if we get sat with someone we already know, though?' a girl from another tutor group called out.

Piers just shrugged. 'No matter. Take the opportunity to find out something you don't know about them. It's only three minutes, then I'll blow the whistle and all the twos move to the left. You're free to talk about whatever you like, but there are prompts on the sheet on the desk if you get stuck. Everyone clear? OK!' He blew the whistle.

I sat down opposite a girl who I'd seen around but had never spoken to. She was very pale with long dark hair and a leather choker-style necklace. It was decorated with long, spiky studs that frankly looked like a bit of a health and safety concern.

'Hi,' she said, letting her hair fall over her face like she was trying to hide.

'Hey,' I said. 'I'm Grace.'

She nodded but she met my eye only for a second before looking down again. She didn't say anything.

'What's your name?' I prompted. I had a feeling this was going to be a long three minutes.

'Uh . . . Sophie,' she said.

I asked her what subjects she was studying, then told her what I was doing, although she hadn't asked, then we lapsed into silence.

In front of us was the slip of paper with the conversation prompt that Piers had mentioned. I decided we could use it. I turned the paper over.

What was the first song you ever downloaded?

Sophie seemed to perk up at this. 'It was 'Bloodlines' by Long Fresh. That's the only music I ever buy really, stuff by Long Fresh. Do you like them?'

She looked at me so hopefully then that I badly wished I could tell her I loved Long Fresh and that we could have seen out the remainder of the three minutes comparing notes on gigs and album tracks. But, alas, I couldn't do that. I'd heard of Long Fresh, vaguely. In fact, I thought I could just about name enough of their songs to fill the rest of the time. But that wasn't the point. Telling Sophie I liked Long Fresh would have been an outright lie.

'No,' I said. 'I think their music sounds like someone banging a saucepan with a spoon. And all their songs sound the same, really.'

She looked crestfallen. 'Oh,' she said. 'I like them.'

I tried to think of the first song I had downloaded. Surely that would give us a subject to talk about for the rest of the slot. Even if she hated it, it would be something to say. But I just couldn't remember. I've never been into music, really.

'I can't remember the first song I downloaded,' I admitted.

She didn't reply. I couldn't think of anything else to say.

'I can't think of anything else to say,' I said.

'Me neither,' she said, still looking down.

Another thirty seconds of painful silence, and our time was up.

An Actual Bucket

As I approached my next meeting, my enthusiasm for my honesty project wobbled. Surely being honest shouldn't mean I was reduced to sitting in silence? There were so many things I could say, as long as they were the truth. I was determined to have a conversation this time.

My friend-date this time was a girl I'd seen in the canteen, sitting with the drama crowd.

'Hey,' she said. 'I'm Nishka.'

'Grace,' I said.

'Cool.' She nodded and the nod went on a bit too long, like she might have been falling into a trance. There were headphones resting loosely around her neck and she was fiddling with the cord, winding it round her fingers.

'This is pretty lame, huh,' she said when she finished nodding. She looked at her watch. 'Waste of time.'

I was about to agree without thinking; she hadn't even phrased it like a question so it seemed the only acceptable response, but then I thought, what do you actually think, Grace? What is the actual honest truth here?

'I think it's a good idea in theory,' I said carefully. 'But it's quite hard to think of what to say to someone you've never spoken to before.'

Nishka nodded. Then, still not meeting my eye, she reached down and turned over the slip of paper on the desk.

Describe the last trip you took.

'I don't really know what it means by "trip",' Nishka said, 'but the last time I went away with my family we went to France to stay in my cousin's caravan park.'

'Yeah?' I grinned. This was excellent. I had plenty to say on this subject and all of it would be completely honest. 'I went to a caravan park in France once. We didn't actually stay there, we were just passing through. It was the most awful day ever.'

I gave her a full honest account of everything that had happened, from Paddy getting car sick to Dad insisting on speaking French to an old man in a village and accidentally saying 'thank you, nice bottom' instead of 'thank you very much', to what happened when we had to pull over at a caravan park because we all needed the loo and we were totally lost.

'Mum went in first,' I told Nishka, 'and when she came out, I said "Was it OK?" – because you know, you never know when it comes to campsite toilets – and she said, "Not wonderful but we haven't got a lot of choice." So in I go and there are three cubicles. Two of the doors are locked but the one on the end was open, so I went in and

I stopped for a moment because I was looking at a bucket. Like, an actual literal red plastic bucket. And I thought, "Mum wasn't joking when she said it wasn't wonderful." But we'd been in the car for five hours and I wasn't exactly in a position to wait another five hours until we found a non-bucket toilet, so I just . . . got on with things.'

Nishka was looking at me with a mixture of horror and fascination on her face. I took this as a sign of appreciation of my story.

'Anyway,' I went on, 'I came out and I said to Mum, "It really wasn't wonderful, was it? Why would anyone pay to come and stay somewhere where you have to wee in a bucket?" And Mum looked at me a bit funny for a minute and then she said, "It wasn't a bucket?" And I just looked at her and then she started to laugh and she said, "Or rather there was a bucket, in the *cleaner's cupboard* at the end of the row!" And I said, "What, that wasn't just a third cubicle?" And Mum said, "No! Didn't you see the mop?" And so I just stood there while she and my brother and my dad were killing themselves laughing because I had totally just weed in the cleaner's bucket!'

Nishka pulled a face. 'Gross,' she said.

'I know,' I said. 'And the thing is, I did see the mop. I just thought it was some kind of massive toilet brush. I mean, how was I supposed to know? Anyway, after we left the camp site we –'

But I didn't get to tell Nishka about the argument Ollie and I had had about how croissants are made or about how the car had started to smell of burning rubber when we were going up a hill, because Piers blew his whistle and it was time to move on.

'Nice talking to you,' I said with a smile as I stood up.

Nishka did a small but unmistaken eye-roll. 'Yeah. Nice *listening* to you.'

Dogs with Voices

Next, I sat down opposite a boy called Martin who I'd been to school with for several years, but had never properly spoken to.

I'd always admired Martin from afar. He just seemed so relaxed in a detached, independent kind of way. He seemed to be popular exactly because he didn't care whether anyone liked him or not. He was the type of person I wanted to impress because he was cool, but that was unlikely to ever happen, because I was not.

'All right?' Martin said with a smile and a slight nod. He was leaning back in his chair with his hands pushed into the pouch at the front of his hoody.

'Uh yeah, hi,' I said.

'Grace, yeah?' he said.

'Oh.' I was surprised he knew. 'Yeah.'

'So . . .' he said.

'Yeah . . .' I said.

He turned the paper over in front of us. 'Shall we look at this?'

The paper had one question typed in the middle.

What's your favourite film?

'*Fight Club*, I guess,' Martin said, with one of his easy shrugs.

I nodded and we were quiet again for a moment. 'I've not seen it,' I said. 'Sorry.'

Martin smiled. 'No need to be sorry. What's yours?'

I had an answer for this one, all wrapped up and ready to go – the answer that I'd decided on several years ago, that I'd picked out for exactly this purpose – so I could wheel it out, without hesitation any time someone wanted to assess my taste. That answer was *Amélie,* an arty, clever, quirky French film, that I hoped would give people the impression that I too was arty, clever and quirky. Maybe even French too, if I was lucky.

The only thing was, that if I really looked deep into my soul, I couldn't say with any certainty that it actually was my favourite film.

I liked it well enough but then I liked *Home Alone 3* well enough and you wouldn't catch me saying that was my favourite film. So now I had to think: what was my actual, *actual* favourite film? I was alarmed to discover that I'd spent so much time carefully choosing my fake favourite film, I'd never properly considered what the truth was.

'I think,' I said eventually, '*Look Who's Talking Now.* That's definitely in the top five, anyway.'

Martin frowned slightly. 'Huh?'

Of course he hadn't heard of it. Why would he? Why

couldn't I have had better taste? But there was no helping that. Being honest meant letting people see the real me. Even if the real me was a loser.

'*Look Who's Talking Now*,' I said again. 'It's about dogs. Well, it's about this couple who get a dog – two dogs, actually – and in the film the dogs have human voices so we know what they're thinking and –'

Martin smiled suddenly, and he leant forward. 'Oh my god, yeah! With John Travolta. And there's this one scrappy dog who chews all the furniture and then that really stuck-up poodle and they kind of –'

'They start dating!' I laughed at how bizarre it sounded. 'I know, it's so not cool. I just think it's funny. I dunno. Cute.'

'Totally!' Martin said. 'I love that film! Actually, maybe it's better than *Fight Club*?'

'I didn't think you'd like it,' I said.

'Why?'

I thought about the honest answer to this question. 'Because you've always seemed really cool and I can't imagine you sitting down to watch a silly little kids' film about dogs.'

He laughed. 'Cool?'

'Yeah,' I said. 'You know . . . with your hair and your clothes, and that walk you do.'

I swung my shoulders, trying to emulate his relaxed swagger.

'I'm not cool!' he said. 'Maybe I think you're cool?'

I frowned. 'Or maybe you don't.'

'I do!' he said. 'I think we're both cool.' He held out his fist. 'Fist bump?' he said. 'For coolness.'

I groaned. 'I think that is a really cheesy thing to do and I'm a bit embarrassed about people watching us but I'm going to do it anyway because it's seems awkward not to and I don't want to mess things up when we're having this really quite nice conversation.'

Martin laughed as we knocked fists. 'Good reasons.'

Piers blew his whistle. 'Catch you later, Grace,' Martin said with a wink.

Shannon

After the speed-friending session had finished, Til and I went to our lockers together. As we took out our books, Nishka walked past. I smiled at her but she didn't smile back. She held her phone up to her ear and put her head down, which is exactly what I do when I see charity collectors in the street and I don't want them to talk to me.

'She was one of yours, wasn't she?' Til said, nodding in Nishka's direction.

'Yeah,' I said with a frown. 'I don't think I made a good impression. Maybe I talked too much.'

'What makes you say that?'

'Well, I talked for the full three minutes and she only said one sentence. And I told her I weed in a bucket.'

'I see,' Til said with a smirk. 'Sounds like you probably did then.'

'It's not my fault though! I was giving a totally honest account of a day when lots of things happened and there's a lot to cover when you've committed to telling the whole truth!'

Til laughed. 'Gracie, I think you can be honest without saying every single thought that floats into your head. No offence but you're not that interesting. No one wants to know that much about you.'

'You're probably right,' I said, feeling a bit sheepish. 'I'm still working on the details of the policy.'

Til, Reeta and I headed to the canteen because Til wanted to use the Surprise Fruit Machine, which was a vending machine they'd installed to encourage healthy eating by delivering a random fruit for fifty pence. Most of the time you got a plain old banana or apple but sometimes you'd get lucky and land a mango. Rumour had it that someone once got a whole pineapple, but how it could've got through the flap at the bottom is a mystery to me.

'Oh. Grapes,' Til said, reaching down and taking the plastic tub from the bottom. 'Could be worse, I guess.' Then she turned and faced the wall suddenly. 'Oh god,' she said. 'Hide me.'

'What?' I looked around us.

'It's Shannon,' she whispered. 'I just met her at the speed-friend thing. She's insane.'

I turned around and saw a girl I recognised from the corridors. She was hard to miss. She had very long blonde hair, shoes with heels so high her feet were almost entirely vertical and a huge white fur coat that made her look like she was giving a piggy back to a polar bear.

As we made our way to a table, Til skulked along with her head down in an effort to avoid Shannon seeing her. It didn't work.

'Oh, hi again,' she called over to us in a strange, drawling voice. I wasn't sure if it was supposed to be American or posh but either way it was very, very false. 'Tilly, wasn't it?' she said, sitting down at the spare chair at our table.

'Til,' Til said.

'These your little friends, are they?' she said, looking at Reeta and me with her nose slightly crinkled, like we were loveable but ugly puppies.

Til nodded but didn't say anything else.

'Grace,' I said. 'And Reeta.' I nodded towards Reeta, who was busy eating from three separate packets of crisps at the same time, stacking them up like little sandwiches before shoving them in her mouth.

We sat in awkward silence for a moment, not quite sure what to talk about now this stranger had joined us. It was clear Til wanted her to leave, but I was willing to give her the benefit of the doubt. I assumed Til was just being grumpy as usual.

'Oh, don't mind me,' Shannon said with a wave of her hand. 'I'm just passing through. Do carry on your chat or whatever.'

She took a tiny mirror out of her handbag, flipped it open and started examining herself in it, flicking her hair back and forth, then reapplying a dark red lipstick.

'So I have news,' Reeta said, doing as Shannon had suggested and ignoring her presence at our table. 'I'm an athlete!'

'I know, mate,' Til said. 'Four cross-country runs a week. Impressive.'

'No, silly!' Reeta said, putting a handful of crisps in her mouth. 'I mean officially.'

As she said the word 'officially' a shower of crisp-crumbs sprayed over the table. Shannon recoiled as if it was toxic waste. Til ignored her.

'How do you mean?' Til asked Reeta.

'So you know I did that race yesterday?'

We nodded. All last week Reeta had been eating even more than usual, huge piles of pasta and bananas, due to some race she had on Sunday afternoon.

'It was the Sussex Junior Championship. And I won! OK, I didn't win, I came second overall. But that's OK because . . . drum roll please . . .' She drummed her fingers on the edge of the table. 'The top two are selected to represent East Sussex in the Southern finals!'

'Oh wow,' I said. 'That's brilliant.' I said it automatically, before I could even check if it was a lie. I decided it was fine. I didn't fully understand the ins and outs of how sports championships worked but I knew that winning was good and that Reeta was pleased so it was true enough to say it was brilliant.

'You're a runner?' Shannon asked, looking out from behind her mirror for a moment.

Reeta nodded. 'Eight hundred and fifteen hundred.'

Shannon crinkled her nose. 'Oh,' she said. 'Distance running.' She said the word distance like it was something distasteful. 'I used to sprint. One hundred was my best. I mean, that's proper running, you know? In distance running you can relax a bit. It's more of a jog really. But when you run the hundred metres it's one hundred per cent energy the whole way.'

'Yeah, I used to –' Reeta began.

Shannon cut her off. She was looking at her reflection in the mirror again. 'I was the only person in my club to do a hundred in under ten seconds.'

Reeta frowned. 'Really? But the world record is ten four nine . . .'

Shannon just shrugged. 'I mean, they never *officially* submitted the time, but everyone knew I could do it.' Then she snapped her mirror shut and stood up, hoisting her bag onto her shoulder. 'Anyway, good luck with the running. Plodders, we always called the long-distancers! I've heard the local competition is . . . cute.'

And she sashayed away, flicking her hair over her shoulder as she went.

'Under ten seconds,' Reeta whispered after she'd gone. 'That's incredible!'

'It's not true,' Til said.

'Oh . . .' Reeta looked confused. 'How do you know?'

Til laughed. 'Well, for one, fairly obviously, she is not the one hundred metre world-record holder. And for two, the girl is a pathological liar. I worked that out within thirty seconds of meeting her, when she told me she reckons she won two grand on a scratch card in the shop last week. She said on the way there she'd been feeling sad about all the homeless people, so as soon as they'd handed over the cash, she'd gone right out into the street and started giving it to all the down-and-outs, like some kind of teenage fairy godmother.' Til shook her head and laughed. 'Like they just hand you two grand in cash there and then, right from the till! She needs to do her research if she's going to make up mental stories. Oh, and she also managed to squeeze in the fun "fact" that her dad invented the electric doorbell.'

'Maybe he did?' Reeta said.

Til shook her head. 'Not unless her dad is 219 years old. I looked it up. She's mad, seriously. She probably hasn't run a race in her life.'

Reeta still looked a bit sad. She sighed. 'Anyway,' she said, 'I was quite pleased to get through the regionals. Even if she does think it's some cute competition.'

'It's wicked,' Til said. 'Seriously, mate. Ignore that loon.'

Time to Give Back

On my way out of college, I bumped into Cool Martin and his mates, who also seem quite cool.

'Hey!' he said, holding out his fist for me to bump again.

'Martin,' I said, keeping my hands firmly in my pockets. 'I really like that you say hi to me now but I really don't want to do the fist-bump thing so please will you not ask again? I find it embarrassing.'

Martin looked surprised for a second but then he laughed and lowered his hand. 'We're going to the beach,' he said, nodding towards his friends. 'You want to come and hang out?'

I looked up doubtfully at the sky. The clouds were thick and dark. 'Uh . . . I don't know.'

'Come on.' He grinned and punched me playfully on the shoulder. 'You want to. You're thinking about it.'

I *was* thinking about it. 'I *am* thinking about it,' I said, carefully considering what was true here. 'I like the idea of hanging around with you and your cool mates, because I could take photos of us all and put them on the internet to show everyone that we're hanging out together. And that might make them think that *I'm* cool. But I'm worried that the actual hanging out itself might not really be that fun.'

'It so would,' Martin said. 'I am so much fun.'

Luckily, I didn't need to offend Martin by saying anything more because I remembered something else that was equally true. 'Actually, I have to get home. My dad's making dinner. He does that now, because he's unemployed.'

Martin frowned slightly. 'OK, fair enough. Next time!' And he and the cool mates sauntered off.

When I got home, things were tense.

Dad had tried to make a kind of vegetarian chilli thing involving lots of lentils and beans but I got the feeling from all the swearing and banging of cupboard doors coming from the kitchen that it wasn't going that well. To make matters more chaotic, Paddy had suddenly become very worried about the bulging blue veins on the back of Dad's hands and was lying in the middle of the floor crying about the 'blue worms' he had inside him.

When Dad eventually called us to the kitchen to eat, the room was foggy with the bitter smoke of burnt cheese. The glass dish in the middle of the table was filled with something that looked like what you'd get if you mixed soil with milk.

'Delicious, darling,' Mum said brightly as she spooned the grey sludge into her mouth. I could see she was just trying to make Dad feel that he had a purpose, looking after things at home even though he wasn't going to work every day.

'And only 90p per portion!' Dad said. 'You see, it *is* possible to eat well on a budget. What do you think, Grace?'

I hesitated. It would have been so easy to just say 'Great, thanks, Dad' and I was very tempted to do so. But that wasn't how it worked. Fifty days of honesty wasn't about always taking the easy route.

'It's nice that you made dinner,' I said brightly.

Dad smiled.

'I can tell you're trying to make an effort because you feel guilty about being unemployed.'

Dad's smile fell a little.

'The actual food though . . .' I prodded it with my fork. '. . . is quite unpleasant, I'm afraid.'

Dad frowned. But then he just looked sad and sighed. He nodded but didn't reply.

I did feel a bit guilty. I hadn't been deliberately trying to hurt his feelings. But there was bit of me that was still angry too. I kept thinking about what Ollie had said – about Paddy not knowing about the money issues either. As if that was supposed to make me feel better, being placed in the same category as a three-year-old.

After my feedback on the food, things at the table were awkward. I pushed my dinner around my plate and gave one-word answers to their questions about college.

'We're still in your bad books then?' Dad said after a while.

I just shrugged.

'Look, I'm sorry,' Dad said. 'I know I've let you all down. I'll find something else.'

'It's not about the job,' I said. 'I know you can't help that. I just can't believe you pretended,' I said. 'That's the worst bit. The weeks of lying!'

'Hardly weeks,' Ollie said, rolling his eyes.

'Two weeks,' I said, pointing at him with my knife. 'That's weeks.'

Suddenly Mum put her fork down. 'Enough,' she said. 'That is enough, Grace.'

'What is?'

'You've made your point. I've had enough of this pouting. This acting like a child. You complain that we treated you like a child, but that's how you're acting!'

'Parenting cliché alert,' Ollie muttered.

'Be quiet, Oliver,' Mum said. Then she turned back to me. 'We've always been supportive of you, putting up with your moods when you were doing your exams and letting you blow off steam over the summer. Now it's time for you to be supportive. It's time for you to give back.'

'What am I supposed to give?' I said grumpily. 'I don't have any money.'

Mum sighed. 'Not money. But you can help out. Just . . . be nice. Don't make everything harder than it needs to be.'

'Although . . . you could get a job, really, couldn't you?' Ollie said.

I glared at him. 'What's it got to do with you?'

He shrugged. 'Just saying. I've got one. I had one at your age. Why can't you get one? Why are you so lazy?'

'I could get a job if I wanted one,' I said, taking a sip of my drink to avoid meeting anyone's eye.

'Go on then,' Ollie said, looking at me hard. 'Dare you.'

'Fine.' I put my glass down and met his stare defiantly. 'I'll get a job.'

Who Wouldn't Want Me?

I had actually been contemplating getting a job for a while. It was true that I'd had a fairly lazy summer, and although I had college work to do, I was hardly run off my feet. The money I'd saved when I'd been too busy obsessing about my GCSEs to ever go out was beginning to run out so if I wanted to do anything or go anywhere over the next year I'd need to start earning some money. And I knew it wasn't fair to rely on Mum and Dad, not at my age, not with everything going on.

I was organised in my approach to the task. I made a list of the places in town where I wanted to work, in order of preference, feeling quite confident that I wouldn't have too much trouble landing something in one of the places near the top of my list. I was young, organised, quick to learn ... who wouldn't want me?

I decided I would like to work in one of the quirky little gift shops, selling overpriced but deeply stylish gifts in North Laine. I could help frazzled businesswomen choose the perfect present for their husbands. I could help parents delight their children at Christmas time. I'd probably be asked to help the manager choose new products to stock too, such would be my obvious good taste and eye for what the people wanted. I took a systematic route around town, from the station to the sea, calling in at the places on my list and asking them if they had any vacancies for part-time work.

I quickly realised, however, that things weren't going to be as easy as I'd thought.

Most places simply didn't need anyone at all, but even those that did had lists and lists of demands – did I have customer service experience? Did I have an up-to-date knowledge of babywear trends? Was I familiar with the snow-sports market?

Really? I wanted to ask, just for a Saturday job? But it seemed the casual work market was tough. I realised I might have to lower my expectations. But even once I had, even once I'd resigned myself to the fact that I might have to settle for something a little less glamorous, I still didn't have much luck.

I retraced my route, back from the sea and up towards the station, this time calling in at all the shops I'd rejected on the way down – a piercing studio, a shop selling crystals and 'chanting aids' (whatever they were). A shop that sold nothing but rows and rows of coloured Biros that I thought might make my eyes spin if I stayed inside too long.

I left my details with a few people who promised to mention me to their managers and call me if there was 'anything suitable', but by the end of the morning I felt thoroughly downhearted. I'd assumed that if I wanted a job, it would just be a matter of getting one. I hadn't properly considered the idea that no one would want me. I felt then, I suppose, my first real sympathy for Dad. It must be ten times harder for him, I knew, getting turned down when we were all relying on him.

At college the next day, I moaned to Til and Reeta about my struggles with unemployment. 'How did you get your jobs?' I asked.

Til was still working at the electronics and second-hand computer games shop that she'd worked in all summer. She shrugged. 'I just asked.'

'*I* just asked!' I whined. 'And they just answered. They answered no. Well, actually, they didn't. They asked me a load of questions back – what can I do, what do I know? And I don't know *anything*.' I rested my head on the table and sighed melodramatically.

'Well, there's your problem then,' Til said. 'When I asked for a job, they asked if I knew about games and stuff and I said, yeah. Because I do. So basically, what it is, Grace, is that I'm a better prospect than you. Suck it up.'

I scowled at her. Because she was right.

'I don't know anything,' Reeta said cheerfully. 'I know nothing about anything.'

'Where is it you work, again?' I asked. 'That American barbecue place?'

Reeta nodded. 'The Ranch.' Then she added in an American accent, 'Our grill, your thrill.'

I crinkled my nose. 'Sounds vaguely pornographic.'

'You could ask for a job there?' Reeta suggested. 'They

always need people because it's horrible and everyone leaves all the time.'

'Great,' I said. 'Sounds perfect. Sign me up.'

Til crushed a Coke can in her hand. 'Beggars and choosers, Gracie. Beggars and choosers.'

I groaned. She had a point.

The Ranch

Reeta had a shift at the Ranch after college that day so she offered to take me with her and introduce me to Floyd, the manager.

The Ranch was down one of the less scenic roads in town – lined with dodgy-looking mobile phone repair shops and strange, derelict pubs with boarded-up windows. I'd seen the Ranch's sign before – chunky bull's horns either side of turquoise neon lettering – but I'd never been inside.

It was about six o'clock when we arrived and the restaurant was full of families. Parents trying to keep little kids busy with crayons and balloons tied to the back of the chairs, older kids playing games on their phones. It smelt like chips and barbecued meat, which I suppose was to be expected. The staff seemed to be mostly about our age, darting about the place in red shirts with black aprons over the top, and baseball caps with little bull's horns poking out the sides.

'There's Floyd,' Reeta said, grabbing an apron from a hook and tying it around her waist. She pointed to a man probably a few years older than us with chin-length brown hair tucked behind his ears. He too was wearing the black apron and cap, but his shirt was blue.

'Reeta,' he said when he saw us. 'Thank Christ. Tables four to twelve, please. Things are crazy.'

'This is my friend Grace,' she said, not replying to his instruction. 'She needs a job.'

He didn't hesitate. 'OK, great.' He reached into a cupboard under the bar and took out a form and handed it to me. 'If you can fill this in.'

'Oh, OK,' I said, looking down at the form.

Floyd seemed busy so I decided not to ask any questions. Instead, I put my hand on the door to leave, thinking perhaps there'd be a chance to talk more another day, once I'd filled in the application form.

'You can sit there,' Floyd said, pointing to a small empty table near the window and handing me a pen.

'Oh,' I said. 'I should fill it in right now, should I?'

'Yeah . . .' He looked at his watch. 'Actually, let's do it together. Might as well do the form and the interview in one go. Kill a bird with a stone and all that.'

Floyd sat down opposite me and took the form back off me. He rattled through the questions on the front page, scribbling down my name, address, contact details and availability.

'So just evenings and weekends then?' he said.

'Yeah,' I said. 'I'm at college in the week.'

He nodded and sighed. 'Aren't they all. Never mind. Better than nothing.'

When he turned to the second page of the form, things

got a little more involved. What experience did I have of working in a catering environment? What examples could I give of a time I'd solved a customer's problem? Why did I want to join the Ranch team? He read them all in one go, reeling them off with a sigh like he didn't want to be asking them any more than I wanted to be answering them.

These would have been tricky questions even in ordinary circumstances, but I was well aware that, with my vow of honesty to consider, they could spell the end of my prospects at the Ranch. If it hadn't been for the fifty-day project, I could have probably just about spun something acceptable, listed my fictional attributes – enthusiastic, hard-working, a real 'team player' – but that was not an option for me right now. I was only three days into my pledge. What kind of joke would I be if I abandoned it now?

So, I sat up straight, I looked Floyd in the eye, and I said:

'I haven't ever worked in catering before. I never really wanted to because sometimes other people's leftovers gross me out a bit. I solved lots of customers' problems when I worked in a pharmacy last year. They were always saying "Oh, excuse me dear, where are the plasters?" or "Do you sell fungal nail cream?" and I would, every time, very patiently, take them to the right place, even though everything was very clearly labelled with big letters and I sometimes wanted to say "Are you blind?" But I never did say that because some of them were actually blind. What was the next one? Why do I want to work at the Ranch? Um . . . it's because my parents are skint because my dad lost his job so I need to earn some money to pay for stuff like milkshakes and new

T-shirts. And because I already asked in all the cool shops I wanted to work in but they didn't have jobs so Reeta said I should try here.'

Floyd looked at me, his head on one side. He was peering at me, his eyes narrowed, like he was trying to read my mind. 'So what you're saying is, you're desperate?'

I held my nerve. I'd come this far. There was no point backtracking now. 'Basically, yes.'

His face broke into a wide grin. 'Excellent. So am I. Welcome to the team.' He held out his hand and I shook it. 'Be here tomorrow at six.'

He swept away back into the kitchen with a tray full of half-empty beer bottles.

Although I'd been taken aback by the abruptness of my appointment, and I was still quite hazy on what exactly I'd be expected to do, as I walked home I felt pleased with myself. I'd gone out and got myself a job! I was going to be earning a living! Well, maybe not a *living*, but earning . . . something. I hadn't actually had time to ask how much.

'It looks like I'm going to be bringing in some money,' I told Mum and Dad importantly when I arrived in the kitchen. 'It's time I contributed.'

'Your twenty quid a week isn't going to go far,' Ollie said from where he was fiddling with his laptop at the table.

'You don't know what I'll be making,' I said indignantly. 'It'll be more than that though, I expect.'

'Doubt it,' Ollie said. 'Minimum wage for under eighteens is less than four quid an hour. And you're at college every day so you won't able to work much.'

'Don't be so dismissive, Oliver,' Mum said. Then she came and kissed me on the cheek. 'Well done, darling,' she said, which was kind, if a little patronising. 'But we don't expect you to contribute. If you can earn yourself a little bit of pocket money then that will be a great weight off our minds.'

I didn't like the way she was terming it 'pocket money' – like I would be using it to buy toffees and comics from the paper shop – but I knew that Ollie was right. I wasn't going to be paying the mortgage any time soon.

But still, I told myself, that wasn't the point.

The point was, I'd set out to get a job, and I'd been completely myself during the whole process.

I'd been one hundred per cent honest, and it had worked.

The Student Team

At Coniston College, we had something called the Student Team, which I suppose was a sort of cross between a school council and student union. There were five people on the Student Team, voted for by the other students, and they had to meet once a week or so, to 'represent the student population in matters that concerned them.' According to my tutor, Piers, the main matter that seemed to concern most students was the end of term socials. But he conceded that it was thanks to the Student Team that we had The Patch, the small outside area with picnic tables and grass where people could sit to work or eat without finding themselves in the middle of a football match, which is what was likely to happen if you hung about too long on the main field.

About three weeks into the term, it was announced that it was time for the election for new Student Team members – two students from our year to join the three already appointed from the year above.

As we ate in the canteen that day, Til, Reeta and I were

discussing the Student Team with a boy called Laurence from one of Reeta's classes.

'Why would anyone want to do it?' Til said. 'It's like working for free, man.'

'Yeah yeah yeah, BUT,' Laurence said. 'It's power, right? And you know what comes with great power?'

I frowned. 'Great responsibility?'

Laurence shook his head. 'Nah, mate. What comes with great power is great *fun*.'

We waited for him to expand on this theory.

'My brother's mate, right,' he said, turning a chair around and sitting on it backwards, resting his elbows on the back, 'he was on the Student Team two years ago and he read all this stuff about how animals can be good for mental health and that, so he managed to persuade them to adopt an actual real life *puppy*, to keep in the library, as, like . . . therapy. Just for people to play with, to help them chill out or whatever.'

'Oh shut up oh my goodness they did not!' Reeta said, her eyes wide, her hands clasped to her chest.

'Straight up,' Laurence said. 'Ask anyone. Only thing was, this dog was like the naughtiest little hound ever born, chewing through the wires, weeing everywhere. Even bolted out into the car park once, knocked some first-year girl off her bike. Had to get rid of him after that. Still though, goes to show. Student Team can do whatever they *want*. A right laugh.'

'I kind of thought only weirdos and losers would put themselves up for the Student Team,' I said to Til and Reeta once Laurence had gone.

Reeta shook her head. 'I've heard loads of people saying they're going for it. 'Sunni, Cool Martin . . . that girl with the sprinting world record.'

Til groaned. 'God. Shannon?'

Reeta nodded. 'Yeah. Her. Apparently, she's telling people that if she gets onto the Student Team, she's going to change Coniston into "the college answer to a five-star spa resort".'

'Oh yeah?' Til said without looking up from her bowl of pasta. 'How's she planning on doing that then?'

'Apparently, she's going to put scented candles in every classroom. And she's going to get the canteen to stop doing burgers and start doing olives and sun dried tomatoes and massive slices of watermelon. *And* she says she knows someone who can turn the art cupboard into a steam room.'

'Ha! That's ridiculous,' I said.

Reeta shrugged. 'People are buying it though. I reckon she'll get on.'

The Candid in Candidate

The following day, Til and I arranged to walk into college together so I waited for her at the bottom of her hill. While she made her way slowly down, I checked Facebook and saw I'd been invited to a picnic to watch some girl called Hazel who I'd never liked that much at school complete a ten-kilometre charity run dressed as a cucumber. Without thinking, I hit the 'maybe' response. As soon as I had though, I realised: that was a lie. Just because I'd pressed a button saying 'maybe' rather than saying the actual *word* maybe with my mouth, that didn't make it any less of a lie.

I went to the event page and read people's comments.

Ah sorry Hazel, I'm in France that week!

I'll be there!

I'm going to try my best to make it, just need to check my work shifts.

I thought for a moment, then added my own comment:

I've put 'maybe' because saying 'no' felt a bit harsh but I'm pretty sure I won't be there. I am impressed that you're running ten kilometres dressed as a cucumber, but I don't really think watching you do it sounds that fun so I don't want to come.

I winced a bit as I wrote it. I hoped the bit about being impressed would make up for the rest of it.

'I've had a thought,' I said as soon as Til reached me.

'First time for everything,' she said.

I ignored her. 'I'm going to stand for the Student Team.'

Til frowned. She unwrapped some chewing gum and put it in her mouth. 'Why?'

'Partly because of what Laurence said. Because it might be fun. Because if someone can persuade them to let us have a college puppy, then who knows what else we might be allowed? I might be able to get them to turn one of the science labs into a cinema or something.'

'Doubtful.'

'Maybe. But the other reason I'm doing it is for an experiment. Just to see if I can get people to vote for me.'

'How do you mean?'

I turned to face her. 'Grace Dart,' I said importantly. 'Putting the "candid" in candidate.'

'You what?' Til said.

'That's my slogan,' I said. 'It means my thing is total honesty. That's my manifesto. My strategy.'

'Your fifty-day project still going then?'

I nodded. 'Yep. Seven days crossed off on my chart now, so I want to take things up a level. I need more of a challenge. More of an experiment. And I really think it's going to work. No lies, no stupid promises from me. People will know they can trust me.'

'If you say so,' Til said.

After that conversation, I think Til thought I'd forget about my plans to stand and we didn't talk about it much for a few days. My confidence was growing though. The more I heard about what other people were promising, the more I felt I could offer something that people would notice. So, one afternoon, I quietly went to the office and added my name to the list of candidates.

Laurence, true to his word, was putting himself up. His campaign seemed to have been inspired by the tale of the naughty puppy and he was basing his campaign around the theme of getting back to nature. What had started with an idea to get a couple of rabbits to live at the end of the field seemed to have escalated to a medium-sized petting zoo featuring chickens, gerbils and a goat.

Another boy in the year called Gareth was arguing for the implementation of some kind of military-style discipline and fitness regime, where we'd all have to do thirty press-ups before registration and start wearing military uniforms to classes. It was actually quite scary.

Shannon, however, was in a class of her own with her campaign strategy, sweeping about the place in her fur coat like the White Witch of Narnia. 'We deserve the best' seemed to be her mantra, and the best apparently meant a fully equipped gym, a massage and aromatherapy room, and a complete overhaul of the canteen menu to include fresh organic produce supplied by a local Italian deli. If anyone questioned the likelihood of her being able to pull these promises off, she was quickly able to mention the names of friends' dads or mums' cousins who 'knew someone' or owed her a 'favour'. The way she talked about it, it sounded like she knew every living person south of London, and ninety per cent of them had something useful to provide.

There was to be a week of official campaigning before the election, which would be held on the Friday. We were each tasked with coming up with a one-sentence slogan to appear next to our name on the college website and on the board in the main hall. My slogan was easily the best of the lot. Even Til and Reeta agreed as Til read the others off the college website.

'"Laurence Fairborn: Let nature be our friend". "Gareth Reed: Military discipline, military standards, military quality". What does that even mean?' Til said, pulling a face.

'What's Shannon's?' I asked, peering over Til's shoulder. 'Is she just going with that awful: "We deserve the best" thing?'

'Nope. Worse.' She moved aside and pointed at the screen.

'"Five-star treatment for all-star students",' I read. 'Give me strength. I don't think she even knows what all-star means.'

'You're going to have to step it up though,' Til said. 'You've got this lot promising goats and saunas and overnight six-packs, and what are you promising? To tell the truth?' Til shook her head. 'It's never going to cut it.'

'We'll see,' I said, because I really wanted to see. I knew there was a chance Til was right, but I wasn't sure I was even bothered whether I got onto the Student Team or not. What I was interested in was if I *could* get on. How much honesty did people want? Did anyone really want the truth?

I Won't be Bored

I wanted to tell Sarah about my standing for the Student Team because that seemed like the kind of thing you should share with someone you're seeing, so I went to find her by the bike racks at the end of the day.

'Look,' I said, opening the website on my phone and holding it out to her. 'Look at some of these lines the others have come out with. Beyond ridiculous.'

She scrolled through them. 'Well, they're better than yours!' She laughed. 'At least they say what they're going to do! You're not promising anything!'

'That's the whole point though, isn't it?' I said huffily, taking my phone back off her. 'I'm the only one who's actually saying what I *mean*. I'm being honest that being honest is all I've got to offer them. That's my whole strategy.'

She looked at me with a slightly bemused expression. Then she said, 'OK!' and slipped on her bike helmet. 'Listen, I've got to go but I'll call you later.'

'Got to go where?' I said, still grumpy.

'Bike park. Kian's cousin is over from Munich and there's a sweet new vert we want to show him.'

'Can I come?' I said without really thinking about it. I wanted to be invited more than I wanted to go.

She hesitated. 'Uh . . . sure. I guess? Won't you be bored?'

I thought about this. I thought I *might* be, but then I might not. And I wanted to not be. I wanted to like it there, as Sarah seemed to so much. I wanted to at least try.

'No,' I said. 'I won't be bored. You never invite me to your stuff.'

I wasn't lying, I told myself, by saying I wanted to come. I was trying. I was trying to make it true. Fake it till you make it, isn't that what they say?

'Oh. Sorry. Didn't think you'd be interested. Yeah, come along.'

Sarah talked about the bike park so much, I'd imagined it to be some kind of grand arena, like something you see on one of those obstacle-course game shows on TV, with lots of impressive props and ramps and flashing lights. But when we hauled open the heavy gate, I found we were standing on the edge of what looked like a neglected kids' play park – a lot of concrete lumps in the middle with tatty graffiti on the walls around the edge. I couldn't tell what was part of the BMXing apparatus and what was just fly-tipped junk. And it soon became apparent that the 'sweet new vert' was just another ramp, albeit a slightly taller one than the others.

'Is this it?' I said, looking around me.

'Yep,' Sarah said brightly. 'This is it. There's Bobby.' She began waving and heading over to a boy in a big green hoody. I followed behind and hovered about waiting while Sarah had a conversation with him about something called pegs and cranks that I couldn't really follow.

And that was the pattern that followed for the next twenty minutes or so – me trailing behind Sarah, waiting for her to introduce me, which sometimes she did as an afterthought and sometimes she didn't do at all. I started off trying to be deliberately charming, to get Sarah's friends to like me, but as they realised I didn't have much to say on the topic of BMXs, their expressions glazed over and they turned their attention back to Sarah. In the end, I gave up.

'I'll go and sit over there then,' I said, pointing vaguely in the direction of a low concrete wall along one side of the park.

'OK,' Sarah said, without looking up from the chain she was adjusting.

As I perched on the wall watching them all spinning up and down ramps, I felt myself getting more and more grumpy. Why were the bikes so small anyway? What was the *point* in all that bunny-hopping about? Why were they wheeling past each other and doing high-fives, when all they'd actually managed to do was jump off a minuscule little box? It looked silly, is what it looked. And it looked easy. That's what I decided, as I watched. They were making out like it was some great skill, but there was nothing to it really. I could easily do it myself. I was sure of it.

'You going to give me a go then?' I said, when Sarah wheeled past me.

She looked up, surprised. 'You want a go on the bike?'

'Yeah,' I said. 'Why not?'

'OK,' she said uncertainly, sliding off the back and holding it out to me. 'Take it easy then . . .'

'Well, I don't just want to ride it here, on the flat,' I said. 'I want to do it properly.' I nodded over towards a ramp.

'You want to go on The Cheese?' she said, raising her eyebrows. 'You know, Gracie, it's steeper than it looks. You've never done it before and –'

'How do you know I've never done it before?' I demanded. 'You've never once asked me if I've done it before.'

She raised an eyebrow. 'So you're saying all this time I've been talking about BMXing, you've been secretly a pro, but just haven't got round to mentioning it?'

I shrugged moodily. 'Maybe I am.'

I took the handlebars from her and stalked off towards the ramp. As much as you can stalk when you're pushing a bike that is surely designed for an elf rather than a human person.

I stopped next to the ramp and looked up. I wanted to go down it – that looked fun – but in order to do that, first I was going to need to get up it. Cycling up would be tricky, I thought – I'd need to get up a hell of a speed to have enough momentum to make it to the top. I decided that the easiest thing would be to just lift the bike up there, then walk up the ramp separately afterwards.

What I quickly realised, however, was that I'd underestimated both the height of the ramp and the weight of the bike. I could lift the bike, but to push it entirely onto the top of the ramp I would have needed to lift the whole thing far above my head, and I just didn't have the upper body strength. I wrestled it this way and that way for a few minutes, but I was painfully aware how ungainly the whole spectacle must look. I ignored Sarah's called offer of help and let the bike fall back down to the ground.

I was starting to feel seriously annoyed with this whole business. And annoyed with Sarah that I was having to do something so silly and pointless to impress her. But I wasn't going to give up now. The solution, I realised, was obvious. I would just walk up the ramp, pushing the bike beside me. Mount it, slide down, job done.

I wheeled the bike around to the front of the ramp, placed its wheels at the bottom of the (actually quite steep) incline, and began to push.

Let me tell you something about metal sheets set to an angle of at least thirty-five degrees: when they're wet – which they are when it's been drizzling for a week – they are more slippery than an eel in a Vaseline coat.

My shoes didn't have much in the way of grip (why would they, I'd put them on for college, not mountaineering up skate ramps) so I managed about four steps before I felt them slide backwards, out from beneath me. And as my feet were sliding downwards, the bike, which I was using to steady myself, slid upwards and out to the right, the front wheel spinning around madly. I was reluctant to let go of the handlebars and have the whole bike land on top of me, so I held on.

The result was that as my feet slid down, my hands were pulled upwards and I was left spread-eagled flat on my stomach, across the entire length of the ramp. Then my whole body slid downwards like a dead jellyfish, and the bike rolled into me, painfully grazing the side of my head with one of its unnecessary protruding spikes.

I sat crumpled at the bottom of the ramp, the bike on its side next to me.

Sarah came jogging over. 'Are you OK?' she said. Her eyes were wide but her mouth was twitching like she was trying not to laugh.

'Fine,' I said, holding my hand to my head. 'Apart from, the stupid bike cut my head open.'

Sarah moved my hand away and peered closely. 'I don't think it's bleeding . . .'

'Oh that's all right then,' I snapped. 'As long as I'm not bleeding to death everything's fine.'

Sarah frowned slightly. 'You know, they're not really meant for walking up, the ramps.'

Some boy called Bobby or Jackson or whichever other one it was came over.

'Everyone OK?' he said, eyeing me anxiously like I was an escaped lunatic. 'Bike OK?'

Sarah hauled it up and checked it over. 'Yeah, think so.'

'Oh good,' I said, wiping my hands on my jeans. 'Great. As long the bike's OK. The precious bike.'

I stormed over to the wall I'd been sitting on and snatched up my bag.

'Grace,' Sarah called after me. 'Don't get in a mood.'

I ignored her, walking quickly across the park and out into the road, letting the heavy metal gate crash shut behind me.

How to Be a Waitress

Although I was nervous about starting work at the Ranch, I was looking forward to it too.

From what I'd seen, the people working there seemed young and cool and I thought it'd be fun to work with Reeta. I knew it was a busy place so I hadn't exactly expected a red carpet to mark my arrival, but I thought there'd be some kind of welcome, or at least someone assigned to look after me and show me the ropes.

But actually what happened was this:

I arrived five minutes before my shift. Reeta wasn't scheduled to be working so I was on my own. I saw Floyd, who seemed as stressed and busy as he had the day I'd met him.

'Table for . . . ?' he'd said to me as I'd come in, grabbing a menu from the shelf by the door and holding it towards me.

'Uh no, I'm Grace,' I said nervously. 'Grace Dart? I think I have a shift now?' Suddenly I wasn't sure if I could count on Floyd to have remembered anything about my hurried interview and immediate job offer. Should I have followed things up, asked for some kind of confirmation letter?

He blinked twice, like someone had thrown cold water on him. Then he sighed and shook his head. 'Of course you are. Of course. Sorry.'

He looked at a clipboard that was hanging on a string from a hook on the wall. 'OK,' he said, gesturing to the back third of the restaurant. 'These are yours.'

'Mine?'

He nodded. 'Tables thirty to forty-two. You serve them.'

'Right,' I said. 'OK.'

By 'OK' I meant 'I have heard your instruction' but to pretend that 'OK' meant 'No problem, that sounds fine, I know exactly what I'm doing' would definitely have been a lie.

I realised I really wasn't sure how to be a waitress at all. I mean, on paper it sounded easy enough – ask people what they want and bring it over, right? – but faced with it, with these tables full of expectant customers, I suddenly felt quite uncertain about the whole thing.

But Floyd had scooted off again so it was clear he wasn't up for giving me a quick tutorial on the basics. I stood there, and for a moment I wondered if my best option might be to turn around and walk straight out.

Then a woman caught my eye, a waitress. She was older than the others, probably about fifty. Her hair was streaked with pink and blue and she had colourful bangles jangling on both wrists.

'You all right there, my love?' she said.

'I'm not sure,' I said.

Then, because I was being honest, and also because I didn't

know what else to do, I said, 'I'm meant to be starting work today and Floyd says tables thirty to forty-two are mine but I don't honestly have any idea what to do or where to start so I was just thinking about running away.'

The woman sighed, and put her tray down on a nearby empty table. 'Give me strength,' she said.

At first I thought she was annoyed with me, for being so completely useless, but then she said, 'That man is as much good as a jelly pencil. He does this all the time, drags in waifs and strays from the street and drops them in it.'

I wasn't sure I liked the idea of being seen as a waif or a stray but I didn't like to argue.

'Don't worry, love. I'll sort you out. First things first, you need a uniform.'

The woman told me her name was Julie and she'd worked at the Ranch for 'more years than there are stars' and she was adamant I shouldn't feel bad about not knowing what to do. 'None of them know, really,' Julie said. 'The young ones. All of them just fudging it up in their own sweet way.'

Julie assured me that the essentials were quite straightforward. I just had to ask people what they wanted, then log their table number and order in the screen at the back of the restaurant, which would send the order directly to the kitchen. There was a shelf with a digital sign above it. When one of my table numbers appeared on the sign, I had to collect the meal from the shelf and deliver it.

'OK,' I nodded, starting to relax a little. It sounded simple enough.

'One thing though,' Julie said. 'Don't forget the American accent. Head office have been sending mystery diners in to check on it. They're having a clamp down.'

'American accent?'

Julie nodded. 'Yep. Every conversation you have with a customer, or within earshot of a customer, has to be done in an American accent. Branding, apparently. Make the place authentic or what have you. People have been starting to get sloppy lately though. I mean, everyone knows to do the initial "Hey y'all!" Ranch welcome but after that people were slipping back into their own accents. But that's not the rule! Rule is, every interaction. The idea is that as far as the customers are concerned, you *are* an American. I mean, they know you're not of course, but just because you know Mickey Mouse is just a man in a suit, doesn't mean you want to see him take off his Micky head and scratch his ear, if you catch my drift.'

'I . . .' I began. 'I don't know if I can do an American accent.'

Julie waved her hand. 'Course you can. Everyone can. It's sixth sense, from all the American telly they pipe in. Watch.'

She approached a family who had just sat down. 'Hey y'all!' she said enthusiastically. And Americanly. 'Can I get you folks some drinks while you look at the menu?'

She took their drink orders, asked the toddler if he wanted some crayons, complimented the older child on her coat, all in an American accent. It was fascinating to watch.

'OK?' she said, returning to her English accent, when she came back over to me.

I wasn't sure I was. 'Even if I can do an American accent, I just don't know if I want to. I'll feel so . . . stupid.'

Julie looked at me and shrugged. 'That's the job,' she said. Then she gave me a small push towards my tables. 'You'll be fine, love.'

The Speech

On the day before the Student Team elections, all the candidates had to give a three-minute speech in the main hall, and anyone in our year who was interested could come along.

Normally I would've felt nervous about this kind of thing.

But this time I actually wasn't worried at all. I realised this was because I didn't have to agonise over what was and wasn't the right thing to say, because there was only one thing I could say: the truth. I just had to stand up and say it. Nothing to decide.

On the day of the speech, Reeta and Til accompanied me to the hall, where they would watch with the rest of the audience.

'I like your outfit, Grace,' Reeta said.

I looked down. The other candidates had dressed up for the speech. Gareth had come into college in his full cadet uniform. Shannon was wearing so much make-up she looked like she might be about to appear in a pantomime. Laurence was wearing a strange checked shirt and welly combo that made him look like a vet on his way to help a cow give birth. In contrast, I was wearing a plain white T-shirt and jeans.

'Thanks,' I said. 'I chose it specifically to look like I hadn't given any thought to it but it actually took me ages to put together.'

Animal-lover Laurence, Military Gareth, Five-Star Luxury Shannon and I sat on the stage with the other three candidates from our year. Jocelyn, one of the tutors, sat in the middle and introduced us all, reading our slogans. I was sure I noticed her smile very slightly at mine, which I decided to take as a compliment.

Our brief for the speech was simple – to explain why we wanted to be elected to the Student Team, how we thought we could benefit Coniston College, and what made us right for the job.

The others filled their three minutes with the kind of stuff I'd been hearing all week. Military Gareth talked about introducing 'the type of discipline and standards that no one seems to bother with any more' and 'making people proud of themselves through old-fashioned hard work'. He then punched the air suddenly, making everyone jump.

Laurence's speech started off confidently enough but he ran out of steam halfway through and the second half was him simply listing his favourite breeds of dogs.

Shannon's was even worse. She seemed to be speaking entirely off the top of her head. 'I mean no offence, but college is kind of rank, don't you think? So I want to just make it nice, you know? So for example, get rid of the gross old toilets and put in some nice blue Moroccan tiles

112

and those taps where the water comes down like a little waterfall. Just because it's college doesn't mean it can't be an attractive place, you know?'

When eventually she ran out of random ideas and tapered off, it was my turn.

'I'm Grace,' I said, standing in the middle of the stage with my hands in my pockets, 'and the main reason I'm standing for the Student Team is because I'm doing a kind of honesty project, where I don't tell any lies at all for fifty days. I was interested to know if anyone would vote for me if I was just completely honest or if people would rather vote for big, impressive promises even though they might all be lies. I mean, I could do my best to get nice stuff like a tiny pig to cuddle at lunchtime or a jacuzzi in the toilets or whatever like the others say, but I'm just going to be realistic and say it will probably never happen. The good thing though, is that you'll always know where you stand with me. I won't pretend we're going to try to do something for you if really we're thinking, "No way, you're dreaming." There are other reasons I want you to vote for me too though. I mean, it would make me feel really popular, for one thing, to get more votes than everyone else. I've never been popular. I mean, no one hates me or anything – at least, I don't know about it if they do – but I've only really got two friends in my year at the moment. This isn't a sob story by the way, I'm just being honest. Uh, what else? Oh, I would actually really like to get to be in charge of the end of term socials because then I can have them the way I want and we wouldn't end up having to have some awful prom with fancy dresses, which

113

I would hate. And also, one more thing I just thought of: it's good to have these things to write on your uni application, isn't it? I don't really have any hobbies so I could do with writing that I'd been in the Student Team – I think it will make me look responsible and hard-working. OK. That's it, I think. The end.'

As I took my seat, people started to clap. And maybe I was just hearing what I wanted to hear but I felt sure my applause was louder than any of the others'.

Election Day

The Student Team elections were a serious business, I discovered when I went into college on election day.

The Polling Station (as it was labelled, with a big white sign with tall black lettering) was in the language lab. People had to queue outside, then file in, showing their student ID card at the door (electoral fraud seemed to be a very real concern) and complete the ballot paper, putting a cross next to the name of the person they wanted to vote for. I was surprised to find that, even though I was a candidate, I was allowed a vote.

'Who am I supposed to vote for?' I asked Til and Reeta.

'Yourself, obviously,' Til said, not looking up from her locker.

'Really? Is that allowed? It seems a bit . . . rude.'

'Course,' she said. 'It's expected.'

'Are you going to vote for me? You're going to vote for me, right?'

'Yeah! Yeah, course,' Til said. 'Probably. Yeah, I think so.'

'Hey, Grace?' Reeta said, taking a block of cheese from her locker and biting into it like an apple. 'You know in your speech when you said you had two friends in our year . . . was one of them me?'

'Yeah!' I said. 'Course!'

Reeta beamed.

'I mean,' I added. 'You're not as good a friend as Til, obviously.'

Reeta's face fell.

'No, don't be sad! It's just the truth. I've known Til for years, I've only known you a few weeks. It's to be expected. And the early signs are good. You can be a bit strange but actually I'm growing to like you *more* since I'm getting to know you, not less, so it's all positive so far.'

'OK,' Reeta said, her head on one side as she chewed her cheese. 'OK. Good.'

I wasn't really sure what to do with myself now that voting was underway. When I'd been with Mum and Dad to vote in elections at the polling station in the church on the corner of our road, there'd always been people from all the parties hanging around outside, wearing big cheesy rosettes and big cheesy smiles, trying to be all friendly and chatty, as if they were just nice people and they weren't at *all* trying to encourage Mum and Dad to vote for them. Some of the other Student Team candidates had obviously seen the same thing, because they were loitering around the polling station, handing out leaflets, repeating their campaign slogans and doing mad smiles at anyone who looked at them. Shannon seemed to have totally lost the plot and was floating up and down the corridors throwing handfuls of glitter in the air and saying, 'It's time to make Coniston magical!'

I don't think I would have been much good at these last-minute campaign tactics even if I'd wanted to be, but as it was, I didn't want to be. Because being fake-friendly was just another form of dishonesty.

Instead, I set out on a methodical tour of the whole college building, delivering my campaign speech to as many people as possible. I hovered around, waiting for an opportunity to speak.

'Hi. I'm just pretending to read this poster while I wait for a gap in your conversation so I can cut in to say: I know I don't really know you that well so it's probably a bit rude to ask for a favour but I'd really like it if you voted for me in the Student Team elections today.'

Some people looked at the ground, muttered something about having somewhere to be, but if I managed to keep their attention long enough I would go on:

'It's not that I really want to be on the Student Team particularly – it might even be a bit boring – but I'm testing out this theory that honesty is the best policy, which means I'm trying hard to be honest all the time. I've based my whole campaign around saying the whole truth and nothing but the truth, which frankly means I've been saying a lot of not very interesting things. So if you vote for me and I get on then I think it will show that honesty *is* the best policy and that's good news for all of us. But most of all for me.'

Most people seemed a bit bemused by my speeches and some just wandered off halfway through, but there was one person who seemed impressed: Sophie, the girl who

I had upset by slagging off her favourite band during my awkward first speed-friend meeting.

'So yeah,' I said, as I finished delivering my speech to what had started off as a group of six but was now just Sophie, leaning against a noticeboard, fiddling with a loose thread on her sleeve. 'If you could vote for me, that would be nice.'

Sophie nodded slowly, not making eye contact, and I thought she would probably silently slope away like the rest of my audience. But as I turned to leave she said, 'It was so cool, what you said.'

I turned back round to look at her.

'Sorry it's all a bit of a muddle. Sometimes I get carried away with the honesty thing and just talk and talk and talk and then –'

'I mean in your speech the other day.'

'Oh! Oh. Really?' I couldn't think of anything cool I'd said. It was all very *not* cool. That was sort of the point.

Sophie nodded. 'When you were like "I'm really unpopular, I've got no friends" I liked it. It made me smile.'

I knew I'd quite specifically said *two* friends, not none, and I didn't think I'd ever said I was actually unpopular, but it didn't seem the time to be picky – not when Sophie was in the middle of giving me a compliment.

'It was just the way you said it,' Sophie said with a shy shrug, still not looking at me properly. 'Like it was no big deal. Because, like, I haven't exactly got many friends, and none at all in college, but I feel like I have to pretend I do and that even to my mum I talk about people like they're my friends when I hardly know them. So it was nice, when

118

you were like "I've got no friends". Because I thought . . . I'm not the only one.'

'Oh,' I said with a shrug. 'OK. Glad you liked it, then.'

Sophie nodded and smiled, making eye contact with me for the first time. 'Anyway, I'm going to vote for you. Honesty's got my vote, for sure.'

The Votes are In

The following Monday was the day the results of the election were to be announced.

On the bus that morning, I felt nervous for the first time. This surprised me. I didn't even want to be on the Student Team, so why did I care what names they read out?

I realised that it was because if no one had voted for me, if everyone thought my speech was lame and my tactics weird, then I would have to think that maybe my whole honesty project was a stupid waste of time. In a way, I wished I hadn't set myself such a big challenge.

I was pondering this when the woman sitting behind me started chatting to me.

'Turned cold, hasn't it?' she said, using her sleeve to wipe condensation off the window. 'Was warm, late this year. But turned now.'

'Yeah,' I nodded, looking down at my phone, trying to send out clear 'don't talk to me' signals.

There was a pause and then she started up again, this time loudly complaining about some school kids at the back of the bus, who were playing noisy videos on their phones. It wasn't that I disagreed – they were annoying – but I didn't really want to join in with her old-lady moaning. I didn't want the kids to think I was a moany old lady too. It was embarrassing.

'Anyway . . .' I said cutting her off as I stood up and made for the stairs.

'Oh. This you, is it? Your stop?' she said.

I groaned silently. Or possibly not that silently. Why had she had to ask that?

'No,' I was forced to admit. 'I'm just going to sit downstairs because I don't want to talk to you any more.'

The woman's face moved quickly from shock to hurt to annoyed. 'Oh, right. Like that is it. Fine. Please yourself. Just trying to be friendly. No one knows how to be friendly any more.' She pulled her handbag to her chest and turned huffily towards the window.

I tried to tell myself that even when it seemed harsh, honesty always paid off in the long run. So , for example, perhaps the lady would no longer waste her friendliness on grumps like me, saving herself instead for people truly deserving of her weather-based chat. And that in the end, my honest criticism would do her good.

I couldn't convince myself of this logic though, and by the time I got to college I'd decided that if my honest Student Team campaign was a total failure, then I'd abandon the honesty project altogether.

In the canteen, everyone was talking about the elections,

speculating about what the results might be. I had a feeling that actually people weren't that interested in the Student Team itself, and probably would forget all about it after today, but it was like wondering who might win *The X Factor* – the few moments where you're waiting for the name to be announced are incredibly tense and exciting.

The results were to be announced at the end of lunch by Ralph, a guy from the second year who currently held the office of Student Team chairman.

The other candidates and I stood in a row at the side of the stage, looking out onto an almost-full hall. As Ralph stepped up onto the stage everyone fell silent. Everything felt very serious suddenly. So serious in fact, I started to giggle and had to bite down on my own hand so as not to look like I was disrespecting the official proceedings.

Ralph held up a red envelope. 'Well, this is it,' he said. 'The votes have been counted and double checked. In this envelope, I have the names of the two people from the first year who will represent your year on the Student Team.'

He opened the envelope and took out a card. He paused for dramatic effect, looking down at the audience.

'Shannon Knight!' he shouted.

Til and I looked at each other across the hall and performed perfectly synchronised eye-rolls. And I immediately lost interest in the whole thing. If Shannon was the type of representative the people wanted, then I didn't want anything to do with it.

'And Grace Dart!'

As quickly as I'd lost my interest in the election, I found it again.

I had been chosen. Chosen by the people, on the strength of nothing but the pure, honest, true contents of my head.

Maybe I was biased, but I was sure my name was met with significantly more enthusiasm than Shannon's. And I lapped it up. I found myself smiling around at everyone, nodding appreciatively and waving, like a visiting queen.

Sarah hadn't been in the hall for the results announcement, but she messaged me soon after.

Well done on the election thing. S xx

I looked at the message. On the one hand, it was nice that she'd sent it, but on the other, I didn't like the way she called it the election *thing*. Why did she have to say 'thing', like it was something so pointless, so silly, that she couldn't even be bothered to think what it was officially called?

I scrolled back through the last few messages we'd exchanged. In my head, she'd been funny with me since the incident at the BMX park, but looking through the texts, I was surprised to see that actually, it looked like I was the one being moody.

She'd messaged me after the day at the BMX park to say sorry. She hadn't said specifically what she was sorry for, just:

Sorry you didn't have a good time x

I hadn't replied.

Then later, she'd asked me if I'd wanted to meet. I remembered writing the message I sent back. I'd been walking along and talking to Til at the same time and I'd punched out the reply quickly, without paying proper attention.

Can't sorry

Was all I'd said.

No kisses. No punctuation even. I hadn't realised that was all I'd bothered to write. After that, nothing from either of us for a full day. I felt like I had some making up to do.

I replied straightaway.

Thanks! Shall I come round later? Xxx

I didn't get a response until much later that evening, when I was already in bed.

Sorry didn't see your message. Crazy busy this week. Xx

I replied and asked what she'd been up to, but when I hadn't heard from her half an hour later, I turned out the light and went to sleep.

Trying

'You've looked at your phone twenty-three times in the last ten minutes,' Til said when we were on the bus to college the next morning.

I didn't say anything.

'Seriously,' she said. 'I counted.'

I still didn't say anything.

'Sarah not messaging you back? Lovers' row, is it?'

Suddenly the story exploded out of me – about Sarah being obsessed with riding those stupid little bikes that make you have to pedal with your knees round your chin and the stupid boys in their jeans that showed their stupid bums and how she basically dared me to have a go on a ramp, which of course I couldn't do but actually why would I want to slide down a ramp, I'm not a three-year-old.

Til looked at me with her head on one side. 'Why did you go with her then? I thought BMX was her thing. Why not just leave her to it?'

I shrugged.

'And why did you pretend you could do it? Why pretend

to like it, even? 'Cause you know what, Gracie – that's lying. And I thought you weren't doing that any more?'

'It's not lying,' I said. 'It's trying. I was *trying* to be into what she's into because that's being supportive. But it's hard to be into something that's so totally rubbish and awful.' I breathed out hard. 'I'm *trying* to make it work.'

Til shrugged. 'Maybe trying and lying aren't so different.'

A Lively Imagination

The first meeting of the Student Team was the week after the election announcement, and I actually managed to be late, which almost never happens to me.

'Sorry,' I said, taking my seat in the semicircle of chairs set up at the end of the language lab. 'Sorry I'm so late.' It would have been easiest to give some vague excuse about having to get something from my locker, but that wouldn't have been true so: 'Basically what happened is I had to go to the loo –'

'OK, no worries,' Ralph said.

But I hadn't finished my full and frank apology:

'And just as I got there,' I went on, getting my notepad out of my bag. 'I saw this girl from my art class go in and I don't know her that well – actually I'm not sure of her name, even – and I really didn't want to get stuck having to chat to her at the sinks – or worse, while we were weeing! – so I had to hide around the corner and wait till she came out.'

Ralph blinked. 'Right!' he said brightly. 'Well, thanks for . . . keeping us informed.'

There were five of us in the semicircle. Me, Shannon, Ralph and two others from the second year – a boy called Yann and a girl called Beth.

Ralph did lots of very serious welcomes and introductions and messages about the duties, responsibilities and 'undeniable privilege' of being on the Student Team. I started to wonder if Ralph might be confusing being chairman of the Student Team with being Prime Minister but I tried my best to look interested and polite.

Shannon was sitting opposite me and I found myself watching her, fascinated. She'd taken her big fur coat off, laid it over her lap and was stroking it like a spaniel. She was chewing gum and she kept popping new bits into her mouth, adding to the collection each time. I started to keep count and I realised that at one point she had eight pieces in there. I had no idea how she managed to keep talking – it must've been the size of a tennis ball – but talk she did.

Whatever subject came up, she had a story to tell about it. Usually a story starring her and her seemingly endless skills, achievements and connections.

First, when we were discussing a collection for a boy on the football team who was in hospital after breaking his leg during a match, Shannon told us a longwinded and bizarre tale from her sprinting 'career' about how she personally had uncovered a scandal whereby a number of her competitors were undergoing elective surgery to have springs implanted in their knees to make them run faster, and the only reason the story hadn't made national news was because they'd paid her to keep her mouth shut. No one could be bothered to point out that she wasn't doing such a good job of keeping her mouth shut now.

'Amazing,' Ralph said, obviously keen to move on to the next item on the agenda.

'Unbelievable, you could say,' I muttered under my breath, and I saw Beth, who was sitting next to me, grin.

Later, someone mentioned an idea that had been raised of setting up a stall selling stationery and greetings cards at college, partly to save people the walk into town but primarily to give art students the chance to show their work by turning it into cards that people could buy.

Shannon was keen to offer her services:

'I invented cards,' she said suddenly. We all looked at her and she laughed. 'Well, not invented cards, obviously. But you know how they're shiny on the front? I invented that. The shine. Me and my ex-boyfriend, it was. We basically came up with the potion that you dip the cards in to make them shine. I can't tell you what it is, obviously, but if you want the cards shiny I know what to do.'

Again, there was a pause while we considered what to make of this strange claim. In the end, Ralph just said, 'Great, thanks. We'll let you know,' and moved the conversation quickly on.

When the meeting was over, I stayed behind to help Ralph put the chairs away.

'Your friend's got a lot of stories,' he said. 'A . . . lively . . . imagination.'

I made a face. 'She's not my friend.'

The Social

At the next meeting, we spent a lot of time discussing the design of the pin badges Ralph wanted to get made for us all to wear to identify us as members of the Student Team. I thought the whole thing sounded a bit pointless and, as my honesty vow prevented me from feigning interest in the project, I think I annoyed Ralph when my only contribution to the discussion was 'I don't really care about this'.

Luckily conversation soon moved on to something I was far more interested in: the autumn-term social. I was relieved. I'd been starting to think that the Student Team was going to be all extra work and missed lunchtimes and no fun at all. But planning a social event was something I could get on board with. I expected it would be all about spending someone else's money on a chocolate fountain and hanging about in the hall making paper chains. Lovely.

Ralph said we had a budget to stick to, but apart from that, the college let the Student Team have pretty much total control over what type of social it would be.

'I think we should start by brainstorming an overall

theme,' he said. 'And just to give you new guys a feel for the kind of thing I mean – we did space one year, covered the whole ceiling with a massive black sheet with little holes in where the light could shine like stars. Another time we did cowboys and cowgirls. Umm, what else . . . ? Other stuff we've done is superheroes, 1920s and . . . bread. We did that once.'

'Bread?' I asked.

Ralph nodded. 'Yeah. All bread snacks, bread hats, bread rolls hanging from the ceiling . . . But anyway, let's brainstorm.'

Ralph stood up and went over to the flip chart.

'What ideas have we got? Let's get them all out, then we can see which ones might actually work.'

Shannon, as ever, had a lot to say.

'We should do a ball. A proper formal ball. But not here, obviously that would be rancid.' She made a face as she looked around the room. 'My friend is friends with the owner of the Grand – you know, the best hotel in Brighton – and he said to me I can use the ballroom there any time I like. For free.'

Ralph raised an eyebrow slightly but he obediently wrote 'formal ball' on the board.

'Or,' Shannon said, with a flick of her hair, 'we could do something more modern. Like street dance, you know? So, I know this guy who does all the choreography for the rap videos. Like Kanye West and Jay-Z and all the main ones. He could come here and we could all learn a massive street dance. I met Kanye once and he said I had a really natural street vibe.'

'I literally can't think of anything more awful,' I said, and I wasn't even going out of my way to be honest, it just came out.

Ralph smirked but wrote 'street dance extravaganza' on the board.

'What about food?' Shannon said. 'Whatever we do, I really think we should go high-end with the catering. We –'

Ralph tried to cut in. 'Maybe let's just get the theme before we –' But Shannon wasn't to be stopped.

'Oh my god,' she went on, perched on the edge of her chair now. 'So you know about magic ingredients, yeah?'

'Magic ingredients?'

'Yeah, so like the sauce in Big Macs or the crispy stuff on KFC, all the stuff that makes people want those foods more and more. It's because it's made up of a special combination of ingredients, like all worked out with maths and science and psychology. And there's a special code to know how to make a magic sauce and basically, my mum's friend knows that code. So what I'm saying is, we could ask her to make something for the party and because it would use the code it would be like the most magic food ever. Like, it literally tastes magic.'

Ralph closed his eyes, just for a second, then he breathed out slowly. 'Right,' he said. 'Magic food.'

I laughed suddenly, making everyone look at me. 'What are you talking about?' I said. 'That doesn't even make sense.'

Shannon looked offended. 'Yes, it actually totally does.'

'Anyway,' Ralph said, holding his hand up. 'I'll write

down magic food but let's keep thinking more generally about themes before we get into the specifics of who'll cater, or if we even want food involved.'

When we managed to get Shannon to stop blurting out every single made-up story that came into her head, we agreed that, as it had been almost non-stop rain and wind since college started, it would be fun to hold a tropical desert island summery beach party. Grass skirts, a barbecue and music on steel drums – all that kind of thing.

'Oh yeah actually, do you know what?' Shannon piped up. 'I'm in this band and my friend normally plays the cello but he's got a steel drum.'

'Yeah? What do you do in the band?' Ralph asked. I could tell he was trying hard to make the question sound curious rather than sceptical.

'Violin,' Shannon said, miming a bowing action. 'I'm grade eight. Well, I mean I never actually did grades but I could easily do the grade eight exam if I felt like it.'

Ralph gave Shannon a tight smile. 'I'm sure. OK, yes. Talk to your . . . uh . . . friend with the steel drum. Anyway, let's talk more next time. Keep thinking of tropical ideas, everyone!'

The Non-Fight

That night, I went to see Sarah. Apart from a quick hello-how-are-you-OK-bye at college, it was the first time we'd seen each other since I'd stormed out of the BMX park.

She was sitting at her desk, fiddling with a screwdriver and some piece of metal that looked like a bike pedal. We chatted for a bit about college and coursework and then she said, 'I take it you won't be coming back to the park?'

'No,' I said. 'Probably not.'

She nodded but she didn't reply. She frowned, gouging her screwdriver deeper into the pedal's mechanism.

I sat down on the end of her bed. 'I just don't see the point. It's all so random. I don't understand why the bikes are so small and why everyone's clothes are so baggy and what the point even is of hopping over objects like that. I just don't see the point.'

'OK!' Sarah said breezily, still not looking at me.

That was what she always said. 'OK!' I used to think she was just easy-going, good-natured. I used to like it. But sometimes, like right now, 'OK' just sounded like indifference. 'OK' just sounded like 'Whatever, I don't care what you think'.

'OK?' I said.

'Yep.'

Why couldn't she argue back? Why couldn't she bothered to have an actual conversation with me? I was frustrated and, as ever, that made me carry on ranting, trying to prod a reaction out of her.

'It just seems like an activity for children,' I said, standing up and pacing the room. 'It's all so ridiculous. I mean, can those people not hear themselves when they speak?' I put on a silly American-surfer accent. '"Amazing flow, man!", "Let's catch some air!", "I'll see you on the deck!". It's not a deck! It's not a ship! It's just sliding up and down a ramp for no reason whatsoever. Why don't you all get bikes that are the right size with a saddle in the proper position and actually ride somewhere with a purpose?'

When I stopped speaking I realised I'd picked up a giant pencil saying 'I saw the sunset at Weston-super-Mare' and was waving it around like a wand. There was a short pause, then Sarah sighed – which was about as near to angry as I'd ever seen her – and said, 'Have you come over purely to slag off my interests?'

I looked down. 'No,' I said quietly.

'Good. What else have you been doing?'

I told her about the autumn term social, and I thought I'd make her laugh by telling her about Shannon's ridiculous claims – about the Grand and being mates with Kanye West's choreographer and knowing the recipe for 'magic food'.

I hadn't meant it to sound like a rant this time; I was just trying to make her laugh, to ease the tension.

She didn't laugh though. She just climbed down from her desk and lay back on her bed, looking at the ceiling. 'She's just trying to impress you,' she said calmly.

'Well, she's the opposite of impressive,' I said.

'Give her a break,' Sarah said.

I rolled my eyes. 'Why can't you just admit that sometimes people are idiots? Why can't you just say "God yeah, what a plank"? Why do you have to be so . . . *reasonable* all the time?'

'Would you rather I was unreasonable?' She was still looking at the ceiling.

'Yes!' I said. 'OK, not unreasonable, but just . . . annoyed. Or angry. Or *anything*.'

Sarah turned on her side and looked at me, her head resting on her arm. 'You know, sometimes, Grace, it feels like you're plenty annoyed for both of us.'

I stood up. 'I'm going home now.'

She got off the bed and went back over to her desk. 'OK.'

Honesty Coconuts

At the next Student Team meeting, we carried on talking about our Totally Tropical summer-in-the-autumn party. With the theme decided, we could get on to the business of brainstorming exactly what we were going to do. Once again, Ralph manned the flipchart to note down our ideas.

Some were immediately disregarded (a live python, mandatory bikinis) but most suggestions made it onto the board for consideration: a piñata, a flower necklace making station, cocktail umbrellas, a sandpit, a photo booth. We chatted briefly about holding it somewhere other than the college hall, but Ralph pointed out that, although we were technically allowed to hold it wherever we liked, paying for a venue tended to eat into the budget.

'Unless we can get a special deal,' he said, turning to Shannon. 'What about your friend at the Grand?'

Shannon shifted about in her chair. 'Oh yeah totally,' she said.

Ralph frowned. 'Totally what?'

'Well, I mean, like, we could totally have used the Grand

because she's said I can have it whenever I like but it's all booked up now.'

'When?'

'Well, like . . . always.'

'Booked up every day, until the end of time?'

'Yeah,' Shannon said. 'I mean, it's the Grand, you know?'

Ralph nodded. 'Fair enough.'

Then he said, 'There is something else we have to think about. I always forget: "Coniston's Conscience".'

Beth and Yann nodded knowingly, but Shannon and I looked blank.

Ralph explained that all the social events put together by the Student Team had to have some kind of social-conscience element.

'It doesn't need to be heavy,' he said, 'but we have to think of some way to give it meaning or a message or something. Something so it's not just about decorating the hall and putting music on and having a laugh.'

'I don't get it,' I said. 'What kind of meaning?'

'So, for example, one year at the Christmas party everyone had to bring a shoebox wrapped up and filled with toys and games and we gave them to kids on the children's ward at the hospital. So it could be charity, but it doesn't have to be. Another time, everyone got given a questionnaire that you had to complete by talking to other people at the party – "Find one person who's been to Peru." "Find three people who have an unusual pet." – that kind of thing. The idea was that it got people talking. That's all it is, really. There aren't any rules. It just has to be something that has

138

some good behind it. They wouldn't let us have money for three socials a year otherwise.'

Ralph asked us all to give some thought to what Coniston's Conscience could be this year, and to bring our ideas to the next meeting.

At first, I didn't spend much time thinking about it at all. I thought it was just some box we had to tick to be allowed our money, and that someone else would come up with something boring but painless that we could just bolt on at the end.

But then an idea came to me when I was in bed one night.

Coniston's Conscience this term could be about honesty. I could work it into my project. The social had to feature something good and moral and worthwhile, and wasn't honesty one of the foundations of a good, moral, worthwhile life?

By the time the Student Team met again, my idea was fully formed.

'Honesty coconuts,' I announced to the room.

They looked at me. 'Eh?' said Yann.

'We already talked about the idea of having a piñata, right? And normally they're filled with what? Sweets? Toys?'

Beth nodded. 'My little cousin had one at his birthday party. A big papier mâché horse filled with candy canes. The kids went crazy hitting it down with sticks to get at the sweets.'

'Exactly,' I said. 'So what about if we do that. But instead of one big piñata, we have lots of little ones? Little papier mâché coconut-shaped piñatas, hanging from pretend palm

139

trees, to fit in with the tropical theme. People hit the coconuts down with sticks, smash them open and take out what's inside.'

'And what is inside?' Ralph asked. 'Sweets?'

I shook my head. 'No. That's the key bit.' I sat forward in my chair, excited now. 'That's what I mean by honesty coconuts. What if, in the coconuts, instead of sweets, we have messages. Sort of like a fortune cookie. Only, not fortunes but *truths*. Confessions. Like . . . "My dad thinks I'm going to become a pro footballer but I just want to play the piano".'

Ralph sat back in his chair, his head on one side, thinking.

Shannon made a face and folded her arms. 'But why? What's the point in that?'

I hesitated. Obviously, I had been giving this a lot of thought but I decided to give them the abbreviated explanation.

'Because people are always lying.' I was careful not to look directly at Shannon at this point. 'Not always deliberately, but we're always pretending to think things that we don't really think and like things that we don't really like and sometimes if we just take a moment to be honest, we can . . .'

I trailed off. We can what? I suddenly wasn't sure.

Shannon's arms were still folded but Ralph was nodding slowly. 'Yeah,' he said. 'I get it. I like it. Sort of . . . bonding. Like group therapy.'

I shrugged. 'Kind of, I guess.'

He turned to the rest of the team. 'What does everyone else think? Who votes yes to Grace's honesty coconuts?'

The vote was carried, with only Shannon dissenting.

The Grumpiest Waitress

After my initial nerves, my first few shifts at the Ranch had actually gone relatively smoothly.

The waitressing side of it was quite straightforward really, with the electronic ordering system taking care of so much that most of my job was just about carrying meals from the serving shelf to the customers' tables and then returning the empty dishes when they were done.

Reeta and I had had a couple of shifts together so she'd introduced me to the staff properly and I was getting to know my favourites, like Dougie, who was about seven-foot tall with a huge smile, and Teresa, who always wore sunglasses, even indoors.

The American accent, though, was one of the bits of the job that I hadn't quite got used to. In fact, the Ranch's whole branding strategy of making us act like we were the grilled food answer to Disney made me uncomfortable. It felt stupid. It *was* stupid, surely?

The thing was, I just wasn't sure whose benefit it was for. I knew it didn't matter that I didn't enjoy it, but I was pretty sure the customers didn't either. I would go up to tables, launch into my 'hey y'all how y'all doing this fine day' speech and I would feel myself go pink and they would look at me like either I was a total lunatic or I was making fun of them. It was all truly painful.

After a few weeks of struggling through, something occurred to me: wasn't this whole American happy-go-lucky act actually just one big lie?

I wasn't American. I wasn't happy-go-lucky. So surely, pretending that I was was dishonest?

And if that was the case, it meant one thing: it had to go.

Job or no job, I was on day twenty-four of a fifty-day honesty vow and I wasn't about to break it by pretending to be a cowgirl.

It shouldn't make any difference to my work, I reasoned. I'd still serve people their meals, I'd still be polite. I'd just be doing it as myself. As British, non-cheery, ordinary Grace. I didn't see what was so wrong with that.

'Hey, Grace,' Teresa said when I got to work that evening. 'How was your weekend?' She sighed heavily, for no apparent reason. Teresa always spoke every sentence like it was an enormous effort. Reeta said it was because she was exhausted from partying every night. Which also explained the sunglasses, I suppose.

I thought about her question. I'd given myself a pep-talk on honesty on the bus on the way to work. I had to remember to be vigilant. It was so easy to let things slip.

'My weekend was fine.' I paused. Then I shrugged. 'I'm sorry but I can't think of anything to add to that. There's

142

no point me telling you what I did because it wasn't that interesting, it involves people you don't know and we both know you're only asking to be polite.'

Teresa yawned. 'Yeah. I don't really care. You wanna know about my weekend?'

I shook my head. 'Nope.' Then, feeling guilty, I added, 'Thank you.'

'Thought not.' Teresa sighed again. 'OK, catch you later, Grace.' She wandered off.

As this instance of total honesty in the workplace seemed to have passed without any great catastrophe, I felt more confident about letting the true Grace show her face during the course of my shift.

I began by greeting my first few tables with a simple 'Hi, what can I get you?'. No American accent. No mad smiling. And just as I suspected, no one seemed in the slightest bit bothered. My first few conversations were unremarkable transactions and I delivered customers what they wanted, none of them paying me much attention at all. So far, no lies, no drama, no problems.

However, about halfway through the evening, I began serving an old couple who seemed keen to chat. I knew straight away this was dangerous territory, because as my awkward weather conversation with the lady on the bus had demonstrated, navigating friendly chit-chat without at least a few white lies to smooth the way can be tricky.

After all the usual business of taking drinks orders was done, the man looked at me, a proud smile on his face. 'You know, it's our anniversary,' he said, nodding towards his wife. 'Forty years ago today we tied the knot.'

'Oh, congratulations.' I gave them a smile but then looked down quickly at my notepad. I had a feeling he was going to ask me for a freebie and that was going to make things awkward because the Ranch policy meant I'd have to refuse. He didn't though.

'For our honeymoon, we went to Columbus, Ohio and we had the best steak we've ever tasted, didn't we, Val? Like taking a bite out of butter.'

Val nodded silently, which I took to mean that yes, it was indeed a good steak.

'So when I saw the sign to this place,' the man went on, 'an all-American grill, I said to Val, I said, "We've got to go there for our anniversary, Val, see if we can't find a steak as good as that again!"' He laughed, though I didn't see what the joke was. 'What do you reckon, young lady?' He looked up at me, unfolding his napkin on his lap. 'Do you reckon the Ranch is up to the challenge?'

I sighed. Why did people insist on asking questions? It was so much easier to be honest when no one asked you anything. I took a moment to compose my truthful answer.

'Well,' I began gently, 'the Ranch is certainly famous for its steaks,' ('famous for' doesn't necessarily mean 'good' so no lies here) 'but you must remember that we are a chain restaurant, most of our chefs have had very little training and our steaks are bought from the cash and carry on Shoreham Road. On the plus side though, they're probably about a quarter of the price that you'd pay elsewhere. And, well,' I finished with a shrug, 'some people do come back so they can't be that bad.'

The man looked at me.

'I must say though,' I added as an afterthought. 'I think taking a bite out of butter sounds kind of gross.'

The man blinked. Silent Val frowned slightly. I thought they were both about to get up and walk right out. But instead, the man started to laugh – a big booming belly laugh. Then he clapped his hands together. 'A very good point, young lady. Fair enough!'

In the end, Anniversary Man and Silent Val actually turned out to be a very easy table. When I accidentally kept them waiting for fifteen minutes with no dessert menu and my only excuse was 'Sorry about the wait, I totally forgot about you' they just laughed. When they thanked me for my friendly service and I said 'That's OK, I'm just hoping for a tip' they just laughed again.

That was the thing with honesty, I was noticing. Sometimes people were so surprised by it, they thought you must be joking.

PART 3:

Where people seem offended

A Big Lot of Aliens

On day twenty-seven of the honesty project, I was woken up by Paddy running into my room naked apart from Ollie's bike helmet and a pair of Mum's boots.

'Gracie!' he shouted with his hands on his hips. 'There is a big lot of aliens in the garden right now today!'

I rolled over to look at him. 'What?'

He came over to my bed and pulled the duvet off me. 'Come *now*, Gracie!' he said. 'You have to help me!'

I got up, snatched my duvet back and got back into bed. 'I'll come and play later, Paddy. Go away.'

He stood in the doorway of my room and shouted down the landing. 'Muuuuum! Gracie won't come and see the alien!'

'It's not an alien, Paddy, it's a tree,' I heard her call as she headed across the landing.

She appeared in my doorway.

'Make him stop shouting,' I said, pulling the duvet up to my chin and closing my eyes.

'He's just excited because a tree's fallen into the garden.'

'How do you mean?'

'Didn't you hear the wind in the night?' she said as she tried to wrestle a wriggling Paddy into a T-shirt. 'That old elm tree next door crashed straight through the fence. Got the tree surgeon coming later to get rid of it, but it's going to be a pain to fix the fence.'

Later that day, Mum, Dad and I watched the tree surgeon carve up and tidy away the sorry remains of the fallen tree.

When he was bagging up the last of the branches, Mum picked up her phone. 'I'll text Alison from work,' she said. 'Get the number of the handyman she uses.'

Dad frowned, putting his mug in the sink. 'What for?'

Mum looked up. 'To mend the fence?'

Dad walked over to the window, pushing his hands into his pockets. 'We don't need to get someone in. I can do it myself. It's not difficult to put a fence panel up.'

Mum and I exchanged a look but we both quickly looked away again before Dad turned around. We were both more than aware that Dad's enthusiasm for DIY tended to outweigh his skills in that department. Over the course of my childhood I could remember exploding taps, a doorbell fixed in such a way that it turned off all the lights any time it was used and more than one occasion when a set of wonkily erected shelves had come crashing down in the middle of the night.

'Are you sure, love?' Mum said. 'He's not expensive, Alison says. We could just ask –'

'I said I'll do it!' Dad snapped.

Mum stopped talking, surprised. She opened her mouth

to say something, but I saw her compose herself and think better of it. She really was being very patient with Dad lately.

'I can do it,' Dad said, more gently this time. 'God knows I've got enough time on my hands.'

Mum looked at me again but neither of us said anything. 'OK!' she said cheerily.

The following day, Dad headed out in the garden with two hammers, a drill, a screwdriver, several pieces of wood of different sizes that he'd found in various drawers in the house, a ball of string and, for some reason, an old pillow. Every so often there'd be a noise from out there – a shout, or a drill starting up. Sometimes there'd be a loud crunch followed by swearing and Mum would dart anxiously over to the window. This went on for several hours.

'I wish he'd let me get someone in . . .' Mum said for about the millionth time as she hovered near the window, ducking behind the curtain any time Dad turned around in case he caught her spying on him.

'Just chill, Mum,' I said. 'It's only a fence. How wrong can it go? It literally just needs to stand there, doing nothing. That is a fence's whole job.'

When it was almost completely dark outside, Dad finally came indoors.

'There,' he breathed out heavily, dropping his tool bag by his feet. 'All done.'

'And it all went OK, did it?' Mum asked tentatively, passing him a mug of tea.

'Yeah.' Dad nodded with a small frown. 'Course. It's only a fence, it's not rocket science.'

He took a sip of his drink and Mum gave his arm a squeeze.

The Fence

The next morning I was once again rudely awakened by my unruly family.

This time it was by Mum, knocking on Ollie's bedroom door and hissing, 'Ollie! Oliver! Wake up!'

I dragged myself out of bed to see what could possibly be going on so early. I stood in my doorway with the duvet wrapped around me like a cloak.

'Oh, Grace! Quick!' Mum said when she saw me.

'What?'

'Go outside and hold the fence up!'

'Huh?'

Ollie opened his bedroom door in his T-shirt and boxers, his hair sticking up all over the place. 'What do you want?' he said. 'What time is it?'

'Ollie,' Mum said urgently. 'Get dressed, and take your dad out. Take him for a beer or something.'

Ollie frowned. 'It's like eight o' clock in the morning.'

'Yes OK, a coffee then,' Mum said, flustered. She looked over towards her bedroom door which was shut. 'Just take him anywhere!'

'Why?' Ollie frowned.

There was a noise from Mum and Dad's bedroom.

Mum looked at me, eyes wild. 'Grace. Listen to me. Go outside –'

'I'm not dressed!'

'It doesn't matter, take your duvet. Go outside and where the fence has fallen over, prop it up and hold it there. But do it from the other side so you can't be seen from the house. Do you understand?'

'What? Why?'

'No time,' Mum said. 'Just go, quick!'

It wasn't really like Mum to be all stressy and rushed and to be making strange demands like go outside with your duvet and hold up a fence, so when she gave me a little shove along the landing, I decided not to argue. I just slipped on Ollie's flip-flops by the back door and made my way out to where the fence had very definitely fallen over. Whatever Dad had spent all day doing to it the day before hadn't been enough to get it through the night.

As per Mum's instructions, I lifted the fence into a standing position, then went around the other side so I could hold it in place without being seen from the house. I wrapped my duvet tightly around me to shield me from the cold wind and crouched down on the ground. I hoped whatever Mum was up to wasn't going to take long.

After a few minutes, I heard voices in the drive – Dad's and Ollie's. I couldn't make out what they were saying. Then Mum appeared by the back door.

'OK, that'll do, thanks, Gracie,' she called.

'Can I put it down now?' I called back.

'Yep, all done!'

I carefully lowered the fence panel to the ground and made my way inside, shivering despite my duvet.

'What was all that about?' I said as Mum handed me a mug of tea, although I was starting to figure it out.

Mum sighed. 'As you can see, Dad's expert repairs were somewhat lacking.'

We both looked out to where the fence panel lay sadly on the ground.

'But he's gone out now . . . ?

Mum nodded. 'I got Ollie to get him out the way for a few hours. Marcus should be here in a minute.'

'Who's Marcus?'

'Handyman,' Mum said. 'Hopefully he can get the fence upright and tidy before your dad gets home and he never need know.'

I made a face. This all seemed a bit unnecessary. 'So we're just going to pretend to Dad that his repairs were fine and the fence is as strong as ever?'

Mum nodded. 'That's about the long and short of it, yes.'

I frowned. 'More lying then.'

Mum turned to look at me. 'Listen, Gracie. Your dad's been ever so low since the whole job thing. I'm just trying to save his feelings, OK?'

'But, Mum . . .' My voice came out more whiny than I'd meant it to. 'I'm meant to be being *honest*. Why does everything have to involve lying?'

Mum sighed. 'I'm not trying to corrupt your moral crusade, darling. I'm trying to be a bit sensitive. I'm not asking you to lie. Just don't say anything. No need to mention fences or handymen at all, OK?'

'Fine,' I said huffily. 'I'm going back to bed. But if Dad asks me directly if we have had any outside assistance with the fence I'm afraid I will be forced to divulge the truth.'

'OK, darling,' Mum said, as a van labelled 'Marcus Morris: Handyman' pulled up in the drive.

Confession Collection

With three weeks to go until the Totally Tropical autumn term social, preparations were well underway.

As they had been my idea, I had been put in charge of organising the honesty coconuts. The construction part had been easy – papier mâché wrapped around balloons, which we then painted brown and covered in short strands of string for the coconuts themselves, and tubes of painted cardboard topped with green tissue paper leaves played the part of the trees we'd hang them from – but that wasn't the bit I was most interested in. The important bit was the messages that we'd poke inside the coconuts, through the little hole that we'd left, just big enough for a rolled-up slip of paper.

I had a very specific vision for how it would all unfold on the night.

Taking it in turns, people would enthusiastically beat down the coconuts with a stick, cracking through its fragile papier-mâché shell (to represent the real but easily destroyable barrier between us all) and sending it falling to the floor. The slip of paper bearing the confession would be lying in the debris, so I would step forward to retrieve it, carefully uncurl it and read out the note to the rapt audience. (We hadn't officially agreed that I would be doing the reading but as it had been my idea I felt it was only fair that I should take a central role in the proceedings.)

After I'd read the confession, everyone would be silent for a moment, while they took in what they'd heard, but then they'd start to laugh as something they had privately felt, deep within them, was said out loud for the first time, and they realised that everyone else felt the same way. Then applause would start. And hugging. Maybe even tears, from the really emotional ones.

The only problem was that not everybody was embracing my vision in the way I would've liked.

We publicised the concept of the honesty coconuts along with the posters for the social around the school. We told people this was their chance to get something off their chest, to anonymously tell the truth about something they never thought they'd be able to.

I'd even given a few examples on the poster to help things along:

I don't want to go to university even though everyone's expecting me to.

I say I'm allergic to dogs but really I'm just scared of them.

We repurposed the lockable boxes that had been used as

ballot boxes during the election and positioned them in various secluded spots around college for people to use to submit their confessions. And despite my fears that no one would get involved, we did get submissions. We got lots. When I went to gather them up a few days after the boxes had been put out, I found I had a whole carrier bag full of messages.

Most of them, however, weren't exactly what I had in mind.

I took the bag of papers to the curtained-off area behind the stage to go through them in private. As I'd expected, there were a few people making a joke of the whole thing, people 'confessing' that they were a member of the Royal family or related to Hollywood stars. There were a few that, if true, I felt were a little on the dark side and might spoil the party atmosphere:

I accidentally gave my granddad the wrong pills and now he's dead.

There were a few that I was pleased with, that seemed to have captured the tone I was aiming for and that I thought would work well on the night:

I have to look up how to spell potato every time I write it.

I told everyone I didn't get into uni but really I just don't want to leave my mum yet.

But then there were the angry ones. The ones attacking people – other students mainly – as if this was their first chance to get the venom they'd been holding onto out of their system. I'd honestly had no idea there were so many people out there with a grudge. This kind of thing was the exact opposite of the warm, bonding experience I was aiming for, so I filed them all into a pile I mentally labelled as 'pointless bitching' – a pile which would shortly be transferred to the bin.

I think Jordan Carter's hair looks like straw.

Peta Hinchley smells of sewage.

Why does anyone like Michael???

(I had no idea who Michael was.)

Something I did notice though, was that there was one person who seemed to be the subject of more than a couple of these nasty messages:

Shannon.

The Brutal Facts

I was taken aback by the sheer number of messages that mentioned her. Although she drove me crazy, I thought that as she'd been voted onto the Student Team, I must have been the only one to notice her more annoying habits.

But apparently not.

It seemed I was far from the only one to feel wound up by Shannon's fondness for a made-up story. Nearly every one of the notes made reference to the fact that Shannon was a liar, that everything she said was rubbish and that she thought she was better than everyone else.

Although I felt a certain sense of satisfaction that other people thought the same as I did, it didn't even cross my mind to pass the messages onto Shannon. Saying mean things about someone was one thing, but saying them to their face was quite another. I planned to drop the notes into the bin at the first opportunity, and Shannon would never have any idea what her fellow students thought about her.

Just then, Til appeared, pulling the curtain back with one hand, a huge floppy slice of pizza in the other. 'What you doing behind here?' She crouched down and started rifling through the notes. 'What's all this?'

For a moment, I wondered if I should stop her – was there some kind of confidentiality rule I should be thinking of, like between a doctor and a patient? – but then I realised I'd never promised the confessions would be secret. In fact, I'd quite specifically said that they would be put inside a papier mâché coconut, beaten down with a stick and read out to the whole college.

'Oof,' Til said, coming across my 'pointless bitching' pile. 'Old Shannon's got a bashing.'

'I know,' I said. 'Not really a surprise though.'

We carried on sorting through the papers, me carefully pulling out the high-quality on-brand messages that were right for the touching bonding moment I had planned, Til laughing at the ones that had completely missed the point.

And then, without either of us hearing her coming, Shannon pulled the curtain back and stood over us, silhouetted by the late afternoon light in the hall.

'Oh my god so is this like the confession thing?' she said, taking in the carpet of paper slips around us and bending down to get a closer look.

'Yeah,' I said, quickly trying to gather the papers up. 'But you shouldn't really look. Confidentiality, you know?'

Shannon made a face, 'Er, Grace, I'm like ON the actual Student Team? I have a right to read them.'

She continued picking up random slips of paper and glancing at the messages. I shot Til a look and as discreetly as she could, she slid the 'pointless bitching' pile off the floor and into her pocket. Unfortunately, though, it wasn't discreet enough. By trying to hide them, she'd got Shannon interested.

'What are you doing with those?' she demanded.

'Nothing,' Til and I said at exactly the same time, which even I could see was suspicious.

Shannon looked as us sideways, the top of her lip curling slightly. 'What? What is it? Are they really good? Is someone going out with a lecturer? Has someone confessed to a crime? Who is it? Show me!'

'No, it's –' I was about to make something up. I wasn't even sure what. I'd just see what came out. But then I stopped myself.

This was exactly what I was trying to avoid. The make-life-easier, keep-everyone-ignorant-of-the-truth-and-smooth-things-along lies. It might make things more comfortable in the short term, but maybe it was better for the truth to come out. Maybe it was better if Shannon knew how the world saw her, so she could try to put things right? Anyway, I was twenty-nine days into my project. Over halfway. I couldn't blow it now, not with a bare-faced outright lie. I wasn't going to ruin all my hard work for Shannon of all people.

I sighed. 'It's OK, Til.' I held out my hand. 'Give me the papers.'

'Grace . . .' Til said, looking uncertain.

'It's OK.' I said again. I went over and fished the whole pile out of Til's pocket. I handed them to Shannon.

Shannon looked at me quizzically, then she began to unfold

them one by one. She read each message in turn, dropping it to the floor afterwards.

Her expression was indignant but her cheeks were flushed. Her eyes, I'm sure, were wet.

'Stupid,' she muttered. 'What a load of crap. Who wrote these?'

I shrugged helplessly. 'We didn't ask for names. It's anonymous.'

'Oh look! Ha! Well I know who wrote this one because the stupid cow put her name on it. Well, thanks a lot, Megan Box, I would rather be locked in a cage with a rabid scorpion than sat next to you in English too, actually.'

Til frowned. 'Can scorpions get rabies?'

Once again, my impulse was to smooth this over. Not really for Shannon but for myself. I just wanted to make this whole awkward situation feel more comfortable. I wanted to tell Shannon that it was just a couple of idiots messing around, that it was probably the same person doing more than one submission, that most people didn't think she was a liar and a nutcase and totally, completely and utterly irritating.

That's what I wanted to say. But that wasn't the truth.

The truth was, apparently, that lots of people *did* think it. And, for that matter, I thought it and Til thought it too. That was the truth of it.

Til was obviously feeling as uncomfortable as I was because she started to speak. 'Look, Shannon, don't stress it, man. There are only a few. And there are bitchy ones about everyone so –'

'Til,' I said, cutting her off. She looked at me.

I turned to Shannon. 'The truth is, there were way more bad ones about you than anyone else. And the other truth is, you do lie. And you are annoying. Every time you speak you're basically making something up, and no one really believes anything you say any more, so we've stopped listening.' Now I'd started, the brutal facts were tumbling out of me like a waterfall. 'And no one really wants to be friends with you because when nothing someone says is real, you might as well be friends with a fictional character like Bart Simpson or Cinderella or the furry one with the ears from *Star Wars*.'

Shannon just looked at me for a moment, frozen, her mouth slightly open. For a moment, I thought she might cry. And in a way, that would've been quite interesting because it would've been an actual authentic emotion for once.

But instead a smile slowly crept across her face. Then she started to laugh.

'Grace, you're so funny! So random. *Star Wars*?! What are you talking about? Anyway,' she said, picking up her bag from the floor, 'I just came to say I'm not going to be around for a bit. It's kind of mental but I've got through to the last stages of this new West End show. It's a big new musical. It's all being kept quiet at the moment because it's a totally new idea, where the cast play instruments instead of just singing but I'm up for the lead.'

I sighed. 'Oh yes. Because you can play the violin. Of course you can.'

'Yeah,' Shannon said, shaking her hair back over her shoulders. 'Grade eight standard.'

'Yeah,' I nodded. 'You said. You're a professional violin player and you're about to take the West End by storm. Got it. Fine. Good luck.'

'Thanks.' She flashed us a smile and then she was gone.

A Certain Confidence

By now, I was a few weeks into my job at the Ranch and I was starting to feel a bit more at home there. A few of the others had got wind of the fact I'd dropped the whole how-are-y'all fake American routine but no one seemed too interested in what I was up to. Even Floyd was definitely within earshot a few times but I guess he was still too desperate for staff to start making a fuss about the details.

And actually, my whole approach of one hundred per cent honesty had largely gone on without drama, or even comment, from most customers. The fact was, most customers didn't want anything from me other than to be asked, 'Can I get you anything else?' and to have their food brought out in good time, so there wasn't really much room to go wrong.

It was true that there had been a few tense moments though. One evening, a man kept clicking his fingers every time he wanted my attention, which annoyed me so much I began avoiding the table altogether.

'Didn't you hear me?' he demanded when I couldn't leave it any longer and had to go and see what he wanted.

'Yes, I heard,' I'd told him calmly. 'But I found it rude so I was making you wait.'

The man looked as if he was about to launch into an angry rant but luckily I was saved by his two giggling sons who clearly quite liked seeing their dad getting told off.

Another time, a woman had insisted that her meal hadn't been what she ordered, despite waiting until she'd eaten the whole thing before registering her complaint. I told her that, as she hadn't spoken up sooner, I wouldn't be able to let her eat free of charge. She'd demanded that I pass on her complaint to the manager at once, adamant that he would be on her side.

I paused and turned in the direction of the kitchen, but then I stopped. What was the point?

I turned back to the woman. 'The thing is,' I told her, 'I'm not going to ask the manager because he's very busy and I know that he'll say exactly what I've already told you, because that's the restaurant policy. What I could do is go and stand out the back for two minutes to make you *think* I'm talking to the manager, then come back and say the same thing again, but that's just a waste of everyone's time so I don't think I'll bother, if it's all the same to you.'

The woman had paid and left quite swiftly after that and I doubted she'd ever be back, but I liked to think that my honesty had shown assertiveness and confidence, and that maybe people had a certain respect for that.

However, there was one run-in where I don't think respect featured very highly at all.

Let me tell you about Nick and Nikki.

Nick and Nikki

Nick and Nikki were regular customers at the Ranch. By my fourth week, I'd waited their table five times, so they were practically family.

They were a couple in their mid-twenties and, although I didn't make it my business to know all the customers' names, I knew Nick and Nikki's well, as Nick had made a point of telling about the 'massive coincidence' that he shared a name with his 'one true love' (he actually called her that).

As customers, Nick and Nikki were unremarkable. He was a bit too chatty for my tastes, so I knew more about him than I strictly needed to (he had invented some climbing rope gadget when he was at university, which had made him loads of money and he planned to set up a charity when he had time; he used to live in Canada; he was scared of lizards – every visit I'd pick up some new fun fact) but they tipped well enough and didn't cause me any problems. As a couple, however, everyone at the restaurant found them very amusing.

Nick was very skinny, with a red rash of spots across his

forehead. He dressed smartly but his clothes always seemed a little bit small for him, his bony wrists hanging around the place, giving him the appearance of a man who'd bought his jumpers from the kids' department. On the plus side, he never stopped smiling and seemed to treat Nikki like she was a cross between a goddess and an invalid, pulling out her chair for her, helping her into her coat. I sometimes wondered if he might offer to jump up and cut her steak for her, to save her delicate hands the trouble.

Nikki, on the other hand, was classically attractive. Tall and blonde with hair that was somehow both swishy and smart. Unlike her boyfriend, she didn't tend to go in for smiling much. In fact, she only really had two facial expressions: completely blank and the one-eyebrow twitch. My colleagues at the Ranch who had been there longer than me and knew Nick and Nikki better had a collection of theories that they used to joke about, including that Nick had bought Nikki from a catalogue or that he had built her himself out of spare car parts. The funniest thing about them though wasn't how far out of Nick's league Nikki was to look at, but how much she seemed to hate him.

Once, I'd been near their table when Nick had been animatedly telling her a story about an interview he'd had with a journalist, and she'd cut him off mid-flow. With her arms crossed and not a hint of a joke or smile on her face she'd said, 'Jesus, Nick, get to the point, you can be so boring sometimes.' Another time, she'd made a big show of not wanting dessert, then when Nick's had arrived, she'd said, 'Actually, that looks all right,' and whipped it out from under his nose and set it down in front of herself. Nick had allowed himself only the briefest frown before asking me to get another dessert for him.

But Nikki wasn't going to stand for that. 'We haven't got time to wait for them to make another one. You can get a Curly Wurly from the shop at the station.'

The worst part was that throughout their 'dates' at the Ranch, Nikki would be on her phone, scrolling through some kind of dating app. While Nick was talking, she'd be swiping through photos of men with their tops off and sending little messages, littered with kisses. It was all truly bizarre.

Still, though, honesty policy or no honesty policy, I had no plans to take it upon myself to launch into an analysis of a customer's relationship. There was nothing in my project that required that kind of responsibility.

That is, of course, unless a customer explicitly asked for my input.

It happened the sixth time I met Nick and Nikki.

As always, I was friendly enough to make their visit go smoothly, but I was generally avoiding hanging around them enough to get drawn into any conversations where my honesty obligations may lead me to say anything that might make Nikki's eyebrow twitch.

On this particular visit, Nikki disappeared to the toilet (to look at photos of her online men in private, perhaps) and Nick beckoned me over to the table.

'Grace, I need a favour,' he said in an urgent whisper. He

reached into his pocket, took out a small box and flipped it open. It was a gold ring, with a big red stone in the middle. 'I need you to hide this.'

Strangely, my first instinct was to assume he'd stolen it, and he wanted me to help him cover up his crime.

'But . . . where?' I asked.

'In the garlic bread,' he said. 'When Nikki reaches in, she'll feel it. Then she'll look up, I'll be down on one knee and . . . surprise!'

It was only then that I cottoned on to the situation.

'You're going to propose?' I said. I hadn't meant to sound quite so horrified.

Nick nodded and grinned. 'Yep. Ring in the garlic bread, me down on one knee, rose between my teeth. Romantic or what? What do you think?'

'I . . .' I couldn't find the words for a moment. But then they formed in my head, and such was the honest life I was living, that it meant they had to also form in my mouth.

'I think that's an atrocious idea,' I said, shaking my head. 'Truly one of the worst I've heard.'

Nick blinked. He looked like I'd slapped him. 'Oh,' he said. 'Not the garlic bread then. I just thought it would be a good place to hide it, it could sort of be all nestled in –'

'I think the garlic bread is the least of your problems,' I told him. 'What about the fact that she just doesn't like you?'

Nick looked at me, his mouth opening and closing like a mechanical dinosaur.

'What? She . . .' He laughed once, then stopped abruptly. He looked sad again. 'What do you . . . ?'

I glanced quickly in the direction of the toilets. No sign of Nikki.

I sat down at the table. 'Nick,' I said gently. 'She's so rude to you. She talks to you like you're her butler. Or a dog. Like a dog she doesn't like.'

'No she doesn't!' Nick leant back in his seat, his hands gripping the edge of the table. He shook his head. 'That's just her way. She's got a quirky sense of humour.'

'Nick, I heard her ask you not to kiss her because it felt like rubbing her face in a bag of seaweed.'

He didn't say anything.

'And she doesn't listen to anything you say,' I went on. 'Last week I saw her push her actual *hand* in your actual *face* to stop you telling a story.'

He narrowed his eyes, thinking. 'She does do that . . .'

'And you know she's on her phone the whole time, even when you're sat here at the table?'

He puffed out his chest. 'Yeah, but that's her work. Emails she has to keep on top of.'

'Oh, I'm sorry, I didn't realise she was a professional torso assessor.'

'Huh?'

'She's looking at photos of men, Nick! Really good-looking men with no tops on, and sending them messages when you're right here!'

'I . . . she . . .' Nick shook his head. Then he looked up, above my head. 'Is that true?'

I spun around.

Nikki was standing over me, her blonde hair billowing

behind her in the breeze from the fans like she was a villain in a comic strip, her blue eyes shiny with rage.

'You spying little cow,' she hissed.

'Is it true?' Nick asked for a second time, and for the second time she ignored him.

'I'll get you sacked,' she said, refusing to take her eyes off mine. 'Stupid little kid. What do you know about anything? I'll get you sacked,' she said again.

Then she grabbed her coat and bag from the back of the chair and headed for the door. 'Come on, Nick!' she shouted, and without a moment's hesitation, he dashed out after her.

Listen to Yourself

When we all sat down for the next Student Team meeting, Shannon's seat was empty. As Ralph wondered out loud how long we should wait for her I suddenly remembered her story about auditioning for the West End.

I told the others what she'd said.

'The West End?' Ralph said, raising one eyebrow.

'Playing the violin, apparently,' I said.

'When's she going to be back?'

I shrugged. 'Didn't say. But if she's going to be in a West End show –'

'If,' Yann sniggered.

Ralph flicked through his notebook. 'Well, let's carry on for today, and see if she's here next time.'

She wasn't there next time.

'I guess we have to proceed on the basis she's no longer helping with the Totally Tropical social,' Ralph said. 'What was she in charge of? Music?'

I nodded. 'Yeah, she was going to play the violin . . . apparently.'

'Lucky escape,' Ralph muttered. 'OK.' He sighed. 'We can just make a playlist on one of our phones, hook it up to the speakers.'

After college that day, Sarah asked me if I wanted to go for a walk on the pier with her as we hadn't done anything together for a while. As we walked I told her about Shannon's sudden disappearance and the shirking of her responsibilities. I was mostly trying to fill the conversation so we didn't have to talk about the sort-of argument we'd had in her room.

'Maybe she really had something on,' Sarah said, watching the Turbo Coaster spin round, looking thoughtful.

I sighed. I couldn't be bothered to argue with Sarah's ultra-generous, give-everyone-the-benefit-of-the-doubt attitude today. 'Maybe.'

'Listen, Grace,' Sarah said. She turned to look at me face on.

'What?'

She took one of my hands in hers but then seemed to change her mind and drop it again.

'What?' I said again.

'I'm not . . .' she started. She took a deep breath and tried again. 'I'm not trying to say anything final or make any big statements but what do you think about how it's going?'

I frowned. 'The Totally Tropical social?'

She closed her eyes for a moment and breathed out slowly. 'No, not the social. Between us.'

I took a step away from her and pushed my hands in

my pockets, my coat bunched up around my ears. 'I don't know. What do you mean? How do you think it's going?'

'I'm not sure,' she said quietly.

I waited for her to explain.

'I don't feel like . . . like you actually like me that much.'

'I do!' I said automatically.

She looked at me, searching my face. 'I just . . . I'm just not sure you've got room for anyone else in your life right now.'

'What do you mean? Anyone else other than who? You think I'm self-absorbed?'

She paused, which was all the answer I needed.

I stepped away from her. 'Right. Great. Thanks.'

She tried to put her hand on my arm but I pulled away.

'Well, what do you think, then? Do you want us to keep seeing each other? We don't have to live in each other's pockets but . . . you do need to want to spend time with me. You do need to not find everything I say completely annoying.'

'You're the one who's always busy!'

'What do you think, Grace?' she said again, gently. 'Honestly. That's your thing isn't it? Being honest?'

I leant on the railing and looked down at the sea hitting the metal stands below.

'I think . . .' What did I think? I paused for a full minute at least. Sarah didn't hurry me, or try to say anything. She just waited. I turned to look at her. 'I think this: I think that you have a nice face and I still like kissing you. I think that when I looked at you in the library I thought you seemed a lot older and cooler than me but now I think you're more just an ordinary person. Sometimes I think you're a bit boring and sometimes I think you think *I'm* a bit boring and I don't like either of those things. On the whole though, I like having a girlfriend. I prefer saying "I have a girlfriend" to "I'm a lesbian" – it's a better way of breaking the news. And I think it impresses people. Anyway, the main thing is, it's not like there is anyone else I want to be with, so we might as well stay together for now. Don't you think?'

Sarah looked at me for a moment. She looked confused like I hadn't been speaking English. Then she laughed, shaking her head.

'What?' I said, confused.

She stopped laughing abruptly. 'You weren't messing about when you said you were going to be honest, were you?'

I didn't say anything.

'Jesus, Grace. Listen to yourself. You have just said to me, "You're boring but I might as well stick with you until someone better comes along."'

'I . . .' I started. Had I said that? Maybe I had.

'Well, you know what?' Sarah said, pulling up her hood as it had started to rain. 'I'm not going to hang around to be someone's warm-up girlfriend. I did like you, I really did, even though you can be a pain. But there's self-absorbed and then there's selfish. And cruel. And you just crossed the line.'

She turned and started to walk quickly down the pier, her shoulders hunched against the rain.

'Sarah!' I called after her. 'Wait!'

She stopped, but she didn't turn around. But what could

I say that would make things better but that was still true? 'Come back, I didn't mean it'? I couldn't honestly say that because I *had* meant it.

Just say something, Grace. There must be something you can say that is both nice *and* honest.

'I like your new coat!' I called.

Sarah kept walking.

This Dog's Face

After my argument with Sarah, I went home, sat on the sofa and sulked. From the bus, I'd taken a picture of a band playing in the square outside the shopping centre. I uploaded it to Instagram now, my finger hovering over the caption box. How could I caption this photo honestly?

I'm just uploading this to make it look like I'm having a good time watching this band.

I held back from adding 'because I want to show Sarah I don't need her anyway'. There was only so much honesty I could manage in one go.

While I waited for Dad to make dinner I took my bad mood out on everyone on the internet by posting the unfiltered contents of my head wherever I felt like it.

A girl from my year had just updated her Facebook status:

Some days I just wonder why I bother.

So I added a comment underneath it:

I know you're only posting this to get people to ask you what's wrong, so here you go: What's wrong?

On Twitter, three girls I used to go to school with were tweeting photos and reminiscences about the great time they'd had on a weekend away in Amsterdam. I butted in on the conversation with:

Can't you have this conversation privately instead of doing it in public to impress everyone with what great friends you are?

Back on Instagram, where my photo and caption about my pretend good time had actually picked up more likes than any photo I'd ever posted of me having an actual good time, I saw a girl I used to go to school with had put up yet another photo of her dribbly Labrador and I wrote:

I don't think we need so many photos of this dog. I swear I know this dog's face better than I know my own.

A few seconds later I got a new message from Til:

When you start trolling puppies it might be time to step away from the internet.

I frowned and shoved my phone into my bag. Maybe she was right.

At dinner, Dad seemed a bit more perky than usual, and Ollie asked him if anything had happened on the job front.

'Yes and no,' Dad said, reaching for more salad. 'Nothing definite yet but I've had a telephone interview and they want me to go in in person.'

'Sounds good,' Ollie said, chewing. 'What's the job?'

'Well, it's funny, actually,' Dad said. 'It's at Coniston.'

'What?' I said, forcing myself to swallow fast. 'Coniston College? *Our* college? Where me and Ollie go every day?'

Dad chuckled. 'Yep. The very same.'

'But . . . what do you mean? You can't be a lecturer, you don't know any subjects.'

'Charming!' Dad said, but he was still smiling. 'Not as a lecturer, no. In the main office, admin and management type stuff. I'd be around and about the place though. Maybe we could even have lunch together sometimes!'

'Oh,' I said. 'Right.' I could feel my face had set itself into a frown.

'It sounds great. Don't you think, Grace?' Mum was looking at me expectantly.

I thought about this. 'Honestly?'

'Of course.'

'I do hope you get a job but I'd really rather prefer it if you didn't get a job *there*. I want you to be happy but not if the only way is by coming into my college and embarrassing me.'

Dad breathed out. He wasn't smiling any more. 'I see.'

'Grace!' Mum said.

'What?' I shrugged helplessly. 'I'm just being honest. I don't want Dad coming into my college. No one wants their dad at college!' I turned to Ollie. 'You don't want it either, right?'

Ollie held his hands up and shook his head. 'Makes no difference to me,' he said. 'I just go in to do my course and get out. I'm not there to make friends.'

I glared at him for being a traitor and Dad got up and started tidying the pots and pans away.

'You know, Grace,' Mum said sternly. 'You wonder why we don't share everything with you but when we do you act like a spoilt brat. There's a difference between being honest and being selfish, you know.'

I opened my mouth to argue, but before I could think of anything to say, I realised that it was the second time I'd been called selfish that day. First Sarah, now Mum. Maybe they had a point.

Without saying anything else, I got up and helped Dad load the dishwasher.

Florida Rise

'Apparently,' Til said as she joined me at my table in the canteen the following day, 'Leonie Parker saw Shannon crying on the bus on Wednesday afternoon.'

I squinted. 'Wednesday . . . ?'

'Right after you showed her all the mean notes about her.'

'I didn't show her!' I protested. 'She saw.'

Til made an unimpressed face. 'Whatever. Anyway, it's obvious that you got to her.'

'Why? Why is it obvious?'

'Oh come on, Grace,' Til said, taking my sandwich out of my hand, breaking off a piece and shoving it into her mouth. 'You didn't buy that whole "I couldn't care less act", did you? She was gutted. You could see the tears in her eyes.'

'I think you're being dramatic,' I said. 'She seemed fine. She was probably crying about . . . about anything. It could've been nothing. In fact, I bet they weren't even real tears. I bet they were fake, acted, *lying* tears. A prop for whatever story she was making up at the time. How she once ran into a burning building to rescue an old lady's budgie but wasn't able to resuscitate it or whatever.'

Til shook her head. 'I feel bad, man. Don't you? You should feel bad. She's gone AWOL because you were mean to her.'

'I wasn't mean!' I protested. 'It was all them.' I flung my arm out across the canteen, gesticulating towards the student population in general. 'It was everyone else. They wrote the stuff. I was just the messenger.'

'Well, in this instance,' Til said with her mouth full, 'I think that's just as bad.'

I didn't say anything. It hadn't been *that* bad, had it?

'We should go and see her,' Til said. 'Check on her.'

'See her? Where?'

Til shrugged. 'I dunno. Wherever she is. At her house? In the West End?'

I rolled my eyes. 'She is not in the West End.'

'All the more reason we should go check on her.'

It didn't take too much asking around to find out where Shannon lived – a house on the estate near Til's flat, on a road called Florida Rise.

'I just don't know what we're going to say,' I said to Til as we wove our way through the narrow roads that criss-crossed the hill behind Til's block. 'Shannon opens the door – or her mum or dad or whatever – and then what do we *say*?'

Til shrugged. 'We just say, "Hi are you OK?" Stop making out this is all so hard, would you?'

'Fine,' I huffed. 'You can do the talking then.'

We eventually found Shannon's house on the corner of

185

Florida Rise. It was a narrow grey pebble-dashed lump with chipped brown paint on the window sills. Not really the house of someone with friends at the Grand and in Kanye West's entourage. But then that was hardly a surprise.

I pressed the doorbell but we didn't hear it ring. We left it a while in case it had sounded somewhere out of earshot, deep inside the house, then Til gave up and rattled the letter box.

There was some crashing from the hallway then the door was opened by a woman with her hair tied back into a tight ponytail. She was wearing a washed-out baggy cardigan over grey jogging bottoms. Behind her, a big black dog was jumping up at her back, trying to push her out of the way and make a break for freedom.

'No, Woody!' she shouted, trying to wrestle the dog down by its collar. 'I said no! Down!'

'Yeah?' she said to us. But before we could reply, she turned back into the house and shouted. 'Troy, come and get the dog, will you?'

A boy who looked about eight came out from a doorway off the hall holding an Xbox controller. He took the dog's collar and dragged him back into the room with him, muttering, 'Shut up, Woody,' as he went.

The woman turned back to us. 'Sorry, yeah?'

'Is Shannon here?' Til said.

The woman pulled her cardigan more tightly around her and tied the cord. 'Shannon?' She sounded surprised. 'Yeah. Probably.'

'Can we . . . see her?'

The woman crinkled her nose like she found the idea

186

of us visiting Shannon, or maybe even Shannon herself, somehow unpleasant. 'If you want.'

She stood back to let us through the door and into the hall. The floor was strewn with empty carrier bags, dog toys and cigarette boxes.

'Up in her room.' She nodded towards the stairs. 'First door on the left.'

We thanked her and headed up. As we did so, I saw the woman picking up a cigarette box from the floor, flipping open the lid, and throwing it down again in disgust when she found it empty.

The door to Shannon's room was closed. Til knocked on it. 'Uh, Shannon, mate, you in there?' She sounded awkward. Nervous even.

No reply. I looked at Til and she shrugged, so I gently pushed open the door.

The room inside was simply furnished. Bare, almost. There was a single bed in the middle of the room, neatly made with a woollen blanket rather than a duvet. There was a desk lined with text books, and a plain wooden chest of drawers. There was nothing to suggest a teen girl lived there. Nothing to suggest anyone lived there at all.

'Weird,' Til whispered. I nodded.

We left the room, closing the door behind us and went back down the stairs. We could see the woman and the boy, Troy, in the lounge. He was slumped on a leather sofa. The big black dog was lying on its back on the floor and Troy was resting his feet on its belly as he concentrated on his Xbox game – something that involved repeatedly hitting a wolf with a stick. The woman was sitting next to him, smoking a cigarette and drinking a can of beer, looking blankly at the screen.

I hovered in the doorway. 'Um . . . Shannon isn't there?'

The woman slowly turned to look at us. 'Not where?'

'In her room.'

'She's gone away,' Troy piped up suddenly, his tongue poking out in concentration as he finished killing the wolf.

'Away where?' the woman said but Troy just shrugged.

'She said she had an audition. For a show. In the West End?' I prompted. Surely her family would know about that, if it were true?

The woman laughed loudly. 'Did she now? She lives in a dream world.'

'So . . . you don't think she's gone to an audition?'

The woman shrugged. 'Doubt it. What would they want with a lanky little show-off like her?'

Til and I looked at each other. 'So if she hasn't gone to an audition, then where –?' Til began.

'Give me strength, I do not know!' the woman snapped suddenly, making us jump. 'She'll be back at some point. Knowing my luck.'

Til jerked her head towards the door and I nodded.

'OK, thanks for your time,' I said, and we left.

Big Break

We picked up chips from the shop at the bottom of Til's hill and took them up to her flat.

'Maybe she wasn't lying after all,' Til said, covering her chips with a blanket of ketchup. 'Just because she lies sometimes doesn't mean she never tells the truth. Maybe she has got an audition.'

I shook my head. 'I don't know. I can't see it. Even her mum thought it was rubbish.'

'Her mum clearly hates her though.'

'Yeah,' I said quietly. 'She did seem to.'

I felt sad then. And, for the first time, properly guilty. Maybe I had been too harsh on Shannon.

Later, when Til was sitting on the floor of her lounge sorting out her tool box, I lay on the sofa and scrolled through my phone. A photo of Shannon popped up in my Facebook feed. It showed her on a station platform, her arms outstretched on either side of her, a violin case in one hand.

She'd captioned the photo:

Just arrived in the big smoke for my audition!
#wishmeluck #shannonsbigbreak

'Look.' I slid my phone across the carpet to Til. 'Maybe you're right. Do you think there's really a violin in there?'

Til peered at the photo. Then she shrugged and passed it back to me, and went back to polishing her wrenches.

On the bus home, I looked at the photo again. I wondered who'd taken it. Was it a friend, someone from outside of college? Or had she had to ask a stranger to help? If she really did play the violin, it stood to reason that she was really in the band she'd told us about.

For the first time, I considered the possibility that she really did have this interesting life that we'd all just written off as fantasy. The band, the choreographer friend. Maybe she really *had* invented the stuff that made greeting cards shiny. Someone must have. I'd just never considered even for a moment that her stories were true. But then I'd always imagined her mum as someone glamorous and a bit conceited, someone who adored Shannon, who'd bought her gold-plated dummies and told her she was a goddess from the day she was born. So what did I know about anything?

As I looked at the photo though, I noticed something. Underneath, in small blue letters, the location where she'd uploaded the image was stamped. But it didn't say London, or even one of the suburbs on the outskirts.

It said:

Bodmin, Cornwall

More Suited to the Role

That evening, I was in the kitchen helping Mum make Paddy's dinner when Dad got a call on his mobile. He snatched it up immediately and went out into the garden.

When he came back in, Mum looked up. 'Who was that, love?' I could tell she was trying to sound casual. 'Anyone interesting?'

Dad made a grunting noise. I saw Mum open her mouth to ask something else but think better of it.

Dad sat down at the kitchen table, pulled his laptop towards him and started scrolling through a page.

As Mum walked across the kitchen behind him, I saw her sneak a look at what he was doing. When she saw, she sighed silently.

'Was that call about the Coniston job?' she said gently.

Dad didn't say anything. He just kept scrolling. Mum didn't ask again. I carried on stirring Paddy's scrambled eggs and pretended I hadn't heard the conversation at all.

Fifteen minutes later, when I was trying to get Paddy to aim his food into his mouth instead of down his front, up his nose or into his ear, Ollie came downstairs, looking like he'd just woken up from a nap.

'All right?' he said with a yawn, to no one in particular. He sat down at the kitchen table opposite Dad. 'Hear anything about the job at college? I saw they've taken the advert down from reception now.'

Mum's head snapped round to look at him, keen to hear the answer.

'Gone to a more suitable candidate, apparently,' Dad said grimly. 'Whatever that means.'

'Ah, rubbish,' Ollie said. 'Annoying.'

'Yep,' Dad said, shutting his laptop suddenly. 'Certainly is. Still, I'm sure you'll be pleased not to have your embarrassing Dad around the place, won't you, Grace?'

He didn't look at me when he said it. He just sat there, looking blankly at the wall in front of him, his hands resting on the edge of the table.

'No,' I said quietly. 'I'm not pleased you're sad, actually. Not pleased at all.'

He Lives in a Castle

My walk home from college the following day took me not too far from Shannon's road and I found myself pausing on the corner, looking over towards her house. It had been four days now since she'd last been at college. If she had had an audition, then surely she'd be back by now? Or maybe she was back in town, but the audition hadn't gone well. Maybe she was sitting alone in that bare bedroom, sulking.

I crossed the road and walked up the gravel path to her front door. I rang the bell before remembering it didn't work, and knocked on the glass instead. There were no signs of life or lights inside so I didn't really expect anyone to open the door. I wasn't even sure I wanted them to. I turned around and walked back down the path. Shannon would probably be back in college tomorrow, I told myself, going on and on about everything she'd seen and done in London.

Then, as I was heading away from the house, I heard a voice.

'You again, is it?' Shannon's mum called from the doorstep. She exhaled a cloud of smoke.

I stopped walking and looked over towards her. 'Uh, yeah. Hi, sorry, I was just . . .' I walked back to the house, pausing at the gate.

Shannon's mum had stepped out of the house and was poking some weeds by the wall with her toe. Behind her the front door was open, and I could see down the path into the hallway. Troy was there again, leaning against the banister with no T-shirt on, eating a yogurt by scooping it out of the pot with his index finger.

'I just wondered if Shannon was back yet?' I called from the gate.

'Haven't seen her if she is.' The woman turned to look at me. She stepped back inside the house and leant on the doorframe. She seemed less angry than yesterday. More just tired.

'I saw this photo,' I said. I took my phone out of my pocket and walked up the garden path. When I reached the front door, I showed Shannon's mum the screen.

She peered at it and nodded. 'That's her,' she said, as if I'd asked for help identifying Shannon.

'I know,' I said. 'But . . . I mean, so it looks like . . . she is going to an audition after all?'

The woman just shrugged and stubbed her cigarette out on the wall.

'She's gone to live with Dad,' Troy said suddenly. 'In Cornwall.' He wasn't looking at us; he was trying to get to the bottom of his yogurt pot using his tongue.

The woman spun round. 'What did you say?' she snapped. 'You don't talk about that man in this house and you don't tell lies. You're as bad as her.'

She made a swipe for Troy but he darted out of her way and ran up the stairs. He stopped halfway up and dropped his empty yogurt pot through the gap in the banisters down onto the hallway floor. 'I want crisps,' he said.

'Go and get some from the cupboard then,' Shannon's mum said, her brief flash of anger sliding back into gloominess.

'There aren't any in the cupboard,' he whined. 'Go to the shop.'

'You go the shop, you little rodent,' his mum said. Then she shuffled off into the lounge, leaving me standing on the doorstep, the front door still wide open.

'I can take him to the shop,' I called, not wanting to step into the house uninvited. 'If it helps?'

There was no reply.

'Cool.' Troy jumped down from the middle of the stairs to the bottom with a crash. He grabbed a coat from a hook near the door, hung it from his head like a cape and pushed past me out of the house.

'Shop's this way,' he said, turning out of the gate and starting off down the pavement.

I looked back towards the house. No sign of objection from his mum. 'Back in ten minutes then . . .' I called.

I shut the front door and followed Troy, watching as he picked up a stick and started using it to hit the doors of parked cars. I hoped none of them had alarms that would go off and make this even more awkward than it already was.

'Troy,' I said, trying to sound as casual as possible. 'Did you say Shannon had gone to live with your dad?'

He nodded but he didn't say anything.

'Did she tell you that?'

He nodded again.

'And where does he live? Your dad? In Cornwall?'

Troy shrugged.

'Bodmin?'

He nodded. Then shook his head. Then he nodded again.

'Do you see him a lot?'

Troy said. 'I seen him when I was . . .' He peered down at his hands, then he held up four fingers.

'Four?' I asked. 'You last saw him when you were four?'

Troy nodded firmly. 'But not Shannon. Only me. He doesn't like Shannon so she couldn't come. She stayed at home.'

'Right. And you don't know where he is now?'

'In a castle!' Troy shouted suddenly. 'He lives in a castle!' And then he ran off ahead of me, his arms stretched out in front of him like Superman.

I sighed. It looked like Troy talked about as much sense as his big sister.

Stick It Out

That night I sat at my desk and tried to concentrate on the chapter I was supposed to be reading on profit and loss reports in my Business Studies text book but I'd read the same four sentences six times and I was still no clearer on what they said. I sat back in the swively leather chair Mum had bought me as a present when I started college and looked up at my honesty pledge on the wall in front of me.

Thirty-four of the fifty numbered squares on the chart below it were marked off with a thick black line. Thirty-four honest days done, sixteen to go. More than two-thirds of the way through. It was good progress. I had done well. I was doing well. So why did it suddenly seem so hard? Why now, for the first time, was I suddenly tempted to rip the chart off the wall and bury it in the garden?

I sighed and rubbed my eyes and closed my text book. Then I went and lay on my bed and looked at the ceiling.

First there was Shannon, off who knows where, roaming around the countryside with a violin case, quite possibly upset by something I had said.

Then there was Sarah, not speaking to me because I'd been 'cruel and selfish'.

And then there was Dad, downstairs, miserable and stressed about not having a job and all I'd managed to do was make things worse by saying I didn't want him to work at my college.

I stood up and went over to the chart. I peeled the top two corners away from the Blu-Tack and the chart flopped downwards, hanging loosely to the wall by the bottom edge. But as I looked at it, all pathetic and abandoned, I remembered something:

The despair before the climb.

This is what Mrs Field had called it in English last year, when she was talking about how all stories have a tough point about two-thirds of the way in where the main character almost gives up, but they don't; they stick it out, and that makes the ending all the better.

Maybe, I thought, maybe this is my tough point, two-thirds of the way in. If I can just get through this, it will make the ending all the better. What would have happened if Dorothy had decided the yellow brick road seemed a bit too long and difficult and had wandered off before she made it to Oz? Where would we be if Harry Potter had just said 'You know what, just let Voldemort win if he's so bothered' and had given up on the whole thing?

If I gave up now, the whole thirty-four days would be wasted.

I lifted the top two corners and pushed them back firmly into the Blu-Tack.

WHERE IS SHANNON???

At college the next day, I told Til about the location stamp
I'd noticed on the photo and about what Troy had said
when I'd called round to see if she'd shown up at home yet.

'It is weird, I guess,' she said, looking at the photo again.
'But maybe the audition was just in Cornwall instead of
London?'

'Why say London then?' I said. 'I can understand why
she'd lie about the whole thing but why change a random
detail like that?'

Til shrugged. 'Shannon is random. Anyway, I thought
you hated her. I thought you only agreed to go round her
house with me because I made you.'

'I don't hate her,' I said. 'It's just the whole thing . . . How
her mum is clearly horrible and what you said about seeing
her crying and now her little brother saying that weird thing
about her going to live with her dad . . . I don't know. I just
want to know what's going on.'

Til shrugged. 'Message her. Ask.'

I paused. 'I already have.'

Til raised an eyebrow. 'Yeah? What d'you say? "Are you really at an audition or have you run away because I was a cow to you?"?'

'I just asked how the audition was going. I didn't say anything about Cornwall at all.'

'And?'

I shook my head. 'No reply. She hasn't even read it either. And I tried to call but her phone's off.'

Til looked at me. 'You called her? Wow. You really care suddenly.'

And I think I did. I just kept seeing her face in my head. The way her eyes were filling up when I said that everyone thought she was a liar. And the way I'd said it, in that clear, unemotional tone like facts were facts and it wasn't my fault or my problem if she didn't like them. But I realised that maybe it *was* my fault. And so maybe it was my problem.

All day I kept checking my phone for a reply, but every time I could see that she still hadn't even seen my message.

I thought about the possibilities. Maybe her phone had been stolen. Maybe it was broken or she'd got a new one. But in the back of my mind I kept thinking, what if something else had happened – something bad? It was clear that it was going to take more than a few days away for her mum to feel concerned. If her mum wasn't interested in making sure she was OK, then who else would?

When I got home that afternoon, I went to my desk and opened my laptop. I stared at the blank screen. I opened Google, but what to search for? I couldn't exactly just type 'WHERE IS SHANNON??' and hope for the best.

I ran a few half-hearted searches without much hope of finding anything useful. I tried 'West End musical, violin', 'New musical cast plays own instruments' and a few other combinations to try to find out more about the show she was supposedly auditioning for, but there was nothing that matched. Then I just typed in 'Bodmin, Cornwall', but for no logical reason because knowing that Bodmin was a civil parish in the North Cornwall parliamentary constituency wasn't going to tell me where Shannon was and if she was OK.

At the top of my Bodmin search results page there was an advert:

Trains to Bodmin: Book now save 50%

I paused. How far was Bodmin? I knew it was quite far west, obviously, but it was all the south, wasn't it? It couldn't be that hard to get to. I could pop down there, just check Shannon was OK, and come back on a return train later that afternoon, couldn't I? It would only take a day. It would be worth it, just to put my mind at rest.

I clicked the link to the train website and entered Brighton to Bodmin in the journey planner.

It took nearly seven hours to get to Bodmin.

And cost £117.

By the time I'd worked enough shifts at the Ranch to save that much up, Shannon could be anywhere.

I sighed and closed my laptop. I was just going to have to accept that whatever Shannon was up to was nothing to do with me.

Clayniacs

I tried to stop thinking about Shannon altogether as it didn't seem like there was anything I could do to find her, but I think she must have still been on my mind and that's why the poster in the art room caught my eye.

I'd been working on my canvas for my coursework and I was hanging around by the sink, waiting for a space to wash up my palette and to kill time I was reading the posters and signs on the cork noticeboard. There wasn't much interesting on there – mostly instructions on where to store the brushes or what to do in the event of a fire, a few stupid things like a photo of a cat falling off an ironing board with the slogan 'Mistakes are proof you're trying'. But in amongst all that, in the top-right corner, there was a poster for an upcoming art competition. In big letters at the top, it said:

Schools of the South
Pottery Throw-deo

Underneath this there was a sketch of a cowboy sitting at a potter's wheel, along with more details of the event:

Inter-school pot-throwing finals
6th November
Bodmin Ceramic and Craft Centre

I paused. I'd barely heard of Bodmin before this week and now it was popping up everywhere, harbouring teenage runaways and hosting strange pottery contests.

'Should be good,' a voice said.

I turned around. It was Steve, the art assistant. He wasn't a lecturer, but he helped out in the art room a few days a week. He mostly just seemed to wash up and stack paints in drawers but I'd caught him sketching once and he was actually pretty good.

He nodded towards the poster. 'It's surprisingly exciting, competitive pot throwing,' he said. 'You haven't lived until you've watched nine seventeen-year-olds lined-up at their wheels going head-to-head in an attempt to fashion the most elegant decorative long-necked vase.'

I laughed. 'Fair enough.'

Steve wandered off and started stacking Tupperware tubs at the front of the studio.

At the bottom of the poster, I noticed someone had written:

Come on Coniston Clayniacs!!!

'Coniston Clayniacs . . . ?' I read.

'Yep,' Steve said from the front of the room. 'That's our little team.'

I was surprised that there were enough people at college with sufficient skill and enthusiasm for pot-throwing to be able to put together a competitive team.

'So we're in the competition?'

Steve nodded. 'Oh yes. It's the highlight of the Clayniac calendar!'

'So you're going down there, to Bodmin?'

I suppose it was at this point that the idea started to form.

'Yes, of course!' Steve laughed. 'Not really the kind of competition you can enter over the phone. We'll head down in the minibus on Saturday morning. We go out for a big dinner with the other teams in the evening, then the competition is on the Sunday morning. It's a lovely little weekend.'

I didn't reply for a moment. I was thinking.

Steve left the room for a few minutes and came back with a box of glue pots that he began unloading into a cupboard.

'Are there any spaces, on the team? On the Coniston Clayniacs?'

Steve looked up, surprised. 'Well, yeah. I guess so. There are only three of us. But there were only two last year, so we're getting bigger!'

'How do you join? I mean "I", not "you". How do *I* join?'

Steve put his box down and scratched his head. 'I don't know really, we've never needed a formal application process . . . Just turn up to our next meeting, I suppose? Tomorrow lunchtime, in the clay room.'

To Be Passionate

'You're joining what?' Til said as we were walking home that day.

'The Coniston Clayniacs, they're called. You know, like maniacs, but with clay. I can't work out if the name is genius or –'

'It's awful,' Til said firmly. 'And I'm going to ask the obvious question: why, exactly, are you joining?'

I told Til about the poster I'd seen for the competition and how Steve had told me what a nice weekend away it was.

Til made a face. 'Not being funny, Gracie, but joining a cult of clay lunatics just so you can have a mini-break sounds kind of insane.'

I didn't say anything.

'Where is it, anyway?' she asked.

'The club? Just in the clay room, I think.'

'The mini-break. Must be somewhere pretty amazing if you're going to this much trouble for it. Dublin? Rome? Rio de Janeiro?'

I paused. 'Cornwall,' I said. 'Specifically, Bodmin . . .'

Til abruptly stopped walking and turned to look at me face on. I stood opposite her, looking down at the floor, fiddling with my sleeve.

'Grace!' Til said, putting her hands on my shoulders. 'What? This is Shannon again, yeah?'

I shrugged her off. 'I don't know. Maybe it *is* insane. I just thought that if I could go down there, to Bodmin, I could see Shannon and just check that she's OK and not, like, having a nervous breakdown or something because of me.'

Til raised her eyebrows slightly but she didn't say anything. She started walking again. 'Anyway, since when did you know how to make a pot?'

'*Throw* a pot, Til. That's what you have to say. You throw a pot. The competition is a throw-deo.' I started to laugh. 'It's actually pretty funny, isn't it? Throw-deo – get it? Throw! Deo!'

Til rolled her eyes. 'Whatever.'

'I don't know if I can or not. I might be able to. I don't know. I've never tried.'

Til frowned. 'So you've managed to persuade them to let you join their pot-throwing team, to go all the way to Cornwall with them to take part in some big competition, when you've *never once* done it before? How did you wangle that?'

I just shrugged. 'They don't technically know that that's the situation.'

Til laughed. 'What about the great honesty project then? That gone out the window, has it?'

'No,' I said. 'I never once told a lie. I told Steve I was a massive fan of pot throwing.'

'Which is a lie,' Til said, frowning.

'It's not,' I said, holding my head up and walking purposefully up the hill. 'Just because I haven't previously been a fan, doesn't mean I'm not now. Passions have to start somewhere and they have to start with a *decision* to be passionate. And I have decided I'm going to be passionate about pot throwing.'

The Clay Room

I wasn't completely deluded. I did realise that I wasn't really going to be able to rock up at a national competition for a skill that I had never once tried and fool anyone that I knew what I was doing.

But, I reasoned, that wasn't going to happen.

There was no reason for me to actually take part in the competition. My only aim was to hitch a ride to Bodmin. Once I was there, I'd slink away, find Shannon, check all was OK there, then rejoin the team for the trip back. I felt quite confident that no one would be too concerned about my absence from the competition as, up until yesterday, they didn't even know I would be taking part at all.

However, when I turned up at my first (and what I intended to be my last) meeting of the Coniston Clayniacs, I found out it wasn't going to be as easy as that.

The existing members of the team were already in the clay room when I arrived – two girls I didn't recognise from the year above and, rather surprisingly, Cool Martin.

'Grace!' Cool Martin greeted me with a wide smile. He

raised his hand to do his favourite fist-bump manoeuvre but I gave him a look and he lowered it.

Steve introduced me to the others and explained that I'd be joining the team, which was fine, but then he said, 'So we need to think about which category Grace can take on for Canterbury,' which was not.

'Canterbury?' I asked.

Steve nodded. 'It's the next national competition. In the spring.'

'But what about Bodmin?' I said. 'I thought the competition was in Bodmin?'

Steve nodded. 'Well, yeah. That's the autumn leg. But that's this weekend. Entries are finalised for that one.'

'Oh,' I said, feeling not only disappointed but silly. 'So I won't be taking part in the . . . I won't be coming to Bodmin?' What a ridiculous plan it had been.

'No,' Steve said. 'Sorry, I didn't realise you expected to. I thought you would have realised arrangements for that one would be all done and dusted by now.'

'No,' I said sadly. 'I didn't.'

'She could do high and mighty?' suggested one of the girls I didn't know.

Steve looked surprised. 'Oh. Well, yes. I suppose . . . I just don't know if . . . ?' He looked at me, his eyes narrowed like he was assessing me.

I frowned, confused. 'What's high and mighty?' I asked.

'It's a round of the competition,' Steve explained. 'Everyone has twenty minutes to throw a piece at least sixty centimetres tall. Throwing tall pots is notoriously difficult and no one in our team is quite up to the standard yet so we weren't going to bother fielding anyone for that category at Bodmin this year. But if you think you might be up to the challenge, it might not be too late to submit you . . . ?'

I paused, and looked around at the others' expectant faces. In my head, I pictured my honesty chart on my wall at home.

Just ten days left to tick off. Four-fifths complete. Eighty per cent done.

Do not lie, Grace. Do not say you know how to throw a high and mighty pot.

I shrugged. 'I might.'

Because, as I saw it, I might. I *might* be up to the challenge. I didn't know that I could do it, but I didn't know for sure that I *couldn't*. I had simply never tried. It might well be that I had a remarkable natural talent for throwing very tall pots.

Anyway, all I needed was to convince them for long enough to get me down there. Once we were safely in the West Country it didn't matter whether I could do it or not.

Steve beamed. 'It would be lovely to be able to compete in that category. It's rather prestigious . . . Why don't you show us what you've got, Grace, and we can make a call?' He nodded towards the wheel.

I froze. 'Show you?'

'Yeah! Just knock us up a bottle vase or something, nice and big.' He went over to the wheel and dropped a heavy chunk of clay in the middle of the plate. 'There you go, all yours. Away you go, then!'

I looked around at their faces. I had to think quickly.

I could probably get out of doing a demonstration – make an excuse about a hand-injury or a contagious skin complaint – but not without lying. And, more to the point, if I didn't at least give it a try, they would never let me in the competition. At least, I reasoned, if I had a go, I might get lucky and magically produce something magnificent and imposing. It was a long shot. But then, I had never tried it before. Maybe I *would* be a natural . . .

I stood in front of the wheel, surveying it. The first thing I had to do was sit on it properly. Nothing would give me away as a fraud quicker than if I sat on the rotating wheel bit instead of the chair and began spinning around the room at a hundred miles an hour like I was in a tumble dryer.

I clambered across the little stool like I was mounting a rocking horse and began to tentatively push the pedal by my feet. The lump of clay in front of me started to spin – much faster than I'd anticipated. I hesitated, my hands hovering above it, not quite sure how to begin. Then I breathed out and silently told myself to get a grip. OK, so I hadn't technically ever thrown a pot before, but I knew the general idea. I'd seen *Ghost,* for goodness' sake. I just had to grab the thing.

I took the clay in my hands.

My plan, such as it was, was to let the clay lead the way. I'd see what formed, quite by chance, while at the same time looking quite sure that whatever happened was exactly my creative intention. When it came to art, I decided, it was all about appearing confident.

Things started off calmly enough as I managed to form

a hollow in the centre of the lump by pushing my thumb down hard. My brief had been to create something tall, and fortunately enough, the clay seemed to want to move upwards. For a short time, I actually had quite a neat cylindrical shape in front of me and I started to wonder if perhaps, against all the odds, I did actually have a natural hidden talent as a ceramicist. I wanted to stop, to quit while I was ahead, but Steve was looking at me as if he was expecting me to go further. I pressed on.

This is where things started to go wrong.

As the piece got taller, one side started to stick out further than the rest. This not only made it very difficult to handle, but meant that as the wide edge rotated in my direction, I was forced to lean backwards. So, as well as trying to wrestle with the wild clay in front of me, I was having to lean forward and backwards quickly to keep my body out of its way, like I was on a high-speed rowing machine.

Handling the clay and moving out of its way at the same time required, it turned out, more coordination than I could muster. I never had been much of a multitasker. With one last wobble, the clay made a break for freedom towards me, and I was forced to throw myself from the stool onto the ground to avoid the whole thing smacking me in the mouth.

I lay on my side, breathing hard from all the drama. The remains of my artwork sat crumpled against the wall, the gap in the top sinking slowly closed like the mouth of a sad jellyfish.

'Are you OK?' Steve asked, helping me to my feet.

Cool Martin went over to the wall to retrieve the remains of the collapsed vase and scooped it into the clay bin.

'Yeah,' I said, shaking my hair and smoothing down my T-shirt. 'All fine. That happens sometimes, doesn't it, when you get really into a piece you can find that –'

Steve was looking at me strangely. 'Grace,' he said, 'have you ever used a potter's wheel before?'

I closed my eyes for a brief moment. It was a direct question. The master blow. There was no way I could dodge it without jeopardising the whole vow.

'No,' I said quietly. 'Not technically.'

Cool Martin laughed. 'Wicked,' he said. He held up his hand for a high five and this time I indulged him by participating.

Steve sat down on the edge of a desk, his hands in his pockets. 'So why did you say . . . ?'

'I just really, really want to go to Bodmin,' I blurted out. That was the truth of it after all.

'Oh, really?' Steve frowned slightly and rubbed his forehead. 'Is that what this has been about?'

I nodded and looked at the floor.

'Tell you what,' Steve said. 'Why don't you come as a supporter? We have a few spaces on the minibus. I can see how keen you are so it'll be interesting for you to see what goes on. Then when we're back we can get you going on the wheel and, who knows, by the time Canterbury comes around you might even be ready to join in.'

'Really?'

Steve nodded. 'Absolutely. Meet us in the car park at eight on Saturday.'

I grinned. 'I shall go to Bodmin after all!' I said in a

pretend-Disney accent that even the Ranch would have been impressed by.

'Er, yes. Indeed,' Steve said and I felt myself go pink.

Cool Martin laughed.

PART 4:

Where I go west

They Don't Care

In the two days between spectacularly throwing myself from the pottery wheel and the planned departure of the minibus to Bodmin, I decided I definitely wasn't going, twenty times at least.

There was a big part of me that was quite sure the whole thing was a very strange, very bad idea. I barely knew Shannon. I had no idea what she was up to or where she was. What was it to do with me? So I'd told her some home truths. So she'd looked a bit miffed. Was I getting carried away with this story I'd told myself that she had run away in a state of despair and I was the only one who could put things right?

As I walked into college the Friday before the competition, I planned to find Steve and let him know that I wouldn't be going after all but as I reached the door, I saw someone I recognised in the college car park.

I couldn't place her at first. She was smoking a cigarette and was all bunched up in a big puffy coat. It was only when she looked directly at me and said 'You looking at something?' that I realised who she was.

'Shannon's mum . . .' I said quietly.

A brief look of surprise crossed her face before she set it back into the scowl.

'Yeah. That's right. You were round the other day, weren't you? You seen her yet?'

'Shannon?'

'Yeah.' She sucked on her cigarette.

I shook my head. 'She hasn't been to college. Didn't her brother – Troy? – say she was with her dad . . . ?'

The woman made a noise that was somewhere between a snort and a cough. 'She ain't. We're not in touch with him.'

'Troy seemed to think . . .'

'He's a kid. He don't know anything.'

I didn't say anything for a moment, and Shannon's mum carried on smoking her cigarette, looking around her like she thought Shannon might walk across the car park at any minute.

'Have you . . . called the police?' I said, and immediately felt silly, like someone who had watched too many crime dramas.

Shannon's mum made a face. 'They don't care. She's seventeen. And she's run away before. "She'll be back when she's ready," they'll say.'

She dropped her cigarette on the floor and stepped on it, then she began to walk across the car park, her hands pushed into the pockets of her big coat. 'Tell me if you hear from her, yeah?' she called back over her shoulder.

I nodded and I felt a pang of something – guilt?

sadness? – that Shannon's mum would think that I would be the one Shannon would call.

Or maybe what I was feeling was responsibility. I had caused this; I had to put it right.

I had to go and at least try to find her.

Road Trip

I met Steve, Cool Martin and the girls from the year above (who I found out were called Ava and Ellie) in the college car park at 8 a.m. on Saturday as instructed.

I saw from across the car park that they were all wearing bright yellow T-shirts with green writing across the chests. As I got closer I saw they said:

**Coniston Clayniacs hit the
Bodmin Throw-deo!**

above the same picture of the cowboy making a pot that had been on the poster.

As I approached the minibus, Cool Martin came over to me and passed me one.

'Got a T-shirt for you too, don't worry!'

I made a face as I took it. 'Really? Do I have to? I'm not even doing the competition. And it's kind of ugly.'

Cool Martin grinned. 'So am I and you still like me.'

I took the T-shirt and pulled it on over my hoody. 'There,'

I said. 'And you're not ugly, you're very good looking and you know it. Unfortunately I have taken a pledge of honesty, which requires me to say this out loud.'

Cool Martin laughed and held up his hand for a high five.

'Martin!' I said, exasperated. 'How many times do I have to tell you! No fist bumps. No high fives. They're awkward.'

'So grumpy,' he said, smiling.

'You know, Cool Martin,' I said as we climbed onto the minibus, 'I've always called you Cool Martin in my head but I might have to cut it back to just Martin if you don't stop trying to high-five me.'

Cool Martin shook his head. 'Savage, Grace. You cut me deep.'

Martin took the seat next to me and as we set off out of the car park and towards the motorway, he began to grill me about my honesty project, starting with why exactly I was doing it.

'Because,' I told him, 'lying is the route of all evil. Lying causes all kinds of confusion and mayhem and misunderstanding.'

'What about good lies? Some lies are good lies.'

I sighed. 'It's an experiment, Cool Martin. I don't have all the answers right now. I will report my findings at the end.'

'So what happens when you finish it?' he said, leaning back in his seat and opening a can of lemonade. 'What do you get for doing the whole fifty days?'

'A sense of satisfaction,' I said without looking at him.

'What if you hurt someone's feelings? What if you look like an idiot?'

I shrugged, still looking out the window. 'These are the risks I must take in pursuit of what is right.'

He was quiet for a while, sipping at his drink. Then he said, 'So if I ask you a question now, you have to tell me the honest truth?'

I turned to look at him, my eyes narrowed. 'Do not take advantage of this situation, Cool Martin.'

He grinned mischievously. 'What, like . . . by asking you your Facebook password?'

I glared at him.

'Or by telling you to give me all your money?'

I frowned. 'I think you're confused about what honesty means.'

He laughed. 'Oh yeah. OK, fine. I still reckon I could have some fun with this . . .'

Luckily, Martin's idea of having fun consisted of asking me a long series of would-you-rather questions:

'Would you rather have a hand for a tongue or a tongue for a hand?'

'Would you rather never be able to shout again or have to shout all the time?'

'Would you rather have a bath full of spiders once or cold baths for the rest of your life?'

Which was all very silly but totally harmless. And it certainly helped the travel time pass easily enough.

When we'd been driving for about an hour, my phone rang and the screen told me it was work. I had asked Teresa to cover my shift, but now I suddenly thought maybe this wasn't officially allowed and Floyd was calling to tell me

I should get down there at once. I answered tentatively, well aware that if any questions were raised about my absence, the honesty project prevented me from using any of the standard excuses involving made-up illnesses or family emergencies.

'Hello?'

'Grace, it's Floyd. From the Ranch.'

'Hi, Floyd. Sorry I'm not in but I spoke to Teresa and she was happy to swap. It's just that I had something important to d—'

'We've got a bit of a problem, Grace,' he said.

I shifted in my seat and leant towards the window to try and stop Martin listening in. 'What kind of problem?'

'A complaint problem.'

I frowned, confused. 'About . . . the food?'

'About you. A customer has alleged that you carried out "a vicious verbal attack" on her.' He said the words like he was reading them from a script.

I paused. Had Floyd got me confused with someone else? I'd been called grumpy before, maybe even rude once or twice. But never vicious. 'What? I didn't . . . I mean . . . what?'

'We got a complaint from . . .' Floyd paused while he checked the details, 'a Miss Nicola Hayes, saying that you accused her of . . . various things.'

'I didn't . . . I don't . . .'

Floyd sighed. 'Look, people here heard you, Grace. Don't get me wrong, everyone's saying she's a cow and they're standing up for you, but it doesn't matter what we think about our customers. We can't start telling their boyfriends

223

what we think of them or interfering in their relationships. You've seriously crossed the line here.'

I suddenly realised who he meant. Miss Nicola Hayes. Nick. Nikki.

'OK,' I said, trying to sound calm. I could explain this. Floyd would understand when he knew exactly what had happened, I was sure. 'I see what you mean. But what happened is that Nick asked me directly if I thought it was a good idea for him to propose to Nikki, and what was I supposed to say?'

'You were supposed to say, "I think that's a great idea, just let me know where to hide the ring. And did you know the Ranch does a lovely cowboy-themed wedding?".'

'But that would have been a *lie,* Floyd. All of it!'

'That's tact, Grace. And good business. Because now we've got Nikki Hayes telling her sorry tale all over Facebook and everyone saying they're going to boycott the Ranch.'

'Oh. I see.'

'Oh indeed. And I mean, it's not going to make much of a dent, her and her mates, but it looks bad, you know? It damages the image. And Head Office aren't happy. We've got to apologise.'

I sighed. I didn't want to apologise because I wasn't sorry. And that meant that saying I was would be lying. But it would be OK, I reasoned. I could phrase it in such a way that prevented it being untruthful. 'I'm sorry for the fuss this has caused' or similar.

I sighed. 'OK, I'll write to –'

'No, I mean, *we've* got to apologise,' Floyd said. 'As in

224

the Ranch, officially. And as part of that apology, we have to agree to let you go.'

I paused. My heart was beating fast suddenly. 'You mean, give me the sack?'

I'd never heard of people getting the actual *sack* in real life before. That was something that happened in films. In real life, people got made redundant, like Dad, or offered a deal to come to a quiet arrangement where they took money if they agreed never to come to work again. But I didn't know people got phoned up and actually banned from coming into work again. Getting sacked was like getting expelled from school. This was all too intense.

'But –' I said.

'Sorry, Grace, I've got to go. Come in and pick up your stuff when you can.'

And then he was gone.

I took my phone away from my face and looked down at it in my hand.

'All OK?' Cool Martin asked.

'I've been . . . given the sack,' I told him. 'Just for telling the truth!'

'Wow!' He grinned. 'High five?'

Bodmin

It was just before two when we drove past a sign welcoming us to the historical County Town of Bodmin. By five past two, I realised I had a problem: Bodmin was big.

I'd had in my head that Bodmin – in fact, maybe all places in Cornwall – were tiny villages. At its heart, there would be a pub and a shop and a little village green with a dog running around on it, maybe two or three roads lined with adorable chocolate-box cottages. Everyone would know everyone and if you wanted to speak to someone in the village – or find out if there were any teenage runaways holed up there – you could just ask the first person you bumped into on the street, and they would be able to point you in the right direction.

But Bodmin wasn't like that, not at all. Bodmin was a full-on, actual proper town. I mean, it wasn't as big or as busy as Brighton, but there were shops and bus stops and a whole range of cafes and pubs and restaurants and lots and lots of roads and cars and noise. There was even an Asda, for heaven's sake.

As Steve parked the minibus in a town centre car park and we collected our bags from the back and wandered around stretching our legs and brushing the crisp crumbs off our T-shirts, I realised this wasn't going to be a simple case of calling into the one local shop, giving them Shannon's name, maybe a brief description, and some kindly West Country lady saying, 'Oh yes, I know that young girl. Staying up at the big house, I believe,' and me straight away being able to spot 'the big house' at the top of a nearby hill. I was fairly certain that if I went into Asda and asked if anyone had seen a girl called Shannon I wouldn't get very far.

The plan for the afternoon was to check into our hostel, then meet up with the other pot-throwing teams to go bowling and for pizza. I had planned to duck out of these social plans to concentrate on my mission, but now I wasn't sure if there was any point. My mission was ridiculous. It was never going to work. There was no way I was going to just happen upon Shannon by roaming the streets. I might as well go with the others and at least have some fun after going to all the trouble of getting myself invited down here.

The youth hostel reminded me of somewhere between a farmhouse and a prison, not that I'd been inside either. Martin and Steve were sharing a big room with five Norwegian fishermen. Ellie, Ava and I had a smaller room with a triple-decker bunk bed. With some considerable effort, I climbed up to the top bunk and lay there, pondering what to do. Across the room, Ellie was straddled across a chair, miming the throwing of a pot, refining her moves before the big day tomorrow.

I hadn't spoken to Til about the idea of tagging along with the Clayniacs to Bodmin after my first mention of the competition, the afternoon I'd seen the poster. I'd told myself I just hadn't got round to telling her, but really I knew it was because if there were ever holes in an idea, Til would be the first person to point them out. And the fact was, my plan of coming all the way down to Bodmin and hoping to bump into Shannon somewhere along the way was one big hole.

Still, there I was, 240 miles away from home, sitting on the top bunk in a youth hostel watching a girl I hardly knew pretend to throw an imaginary pot. I was too far into things to give up now. I decided to swallow my pride and call Til for her advice.

As I predicted, she was decidedly unimpressed by my attempts to carry out a detective operation. Or a rescue mission. Whatever it was.

'So,' she said slowly, 'just to confirm: you thought you'd hitch a ride down to Bodmin in the college minibus, then stand in the middle of the road like a town crier shouting, "Shannon! You can come out now! I've come to say sorry!"?'

'Yes,' I said. 'That's basically it.'

I waited patiently while she finished laughing. Sometimes it was easier to take it than to fight it.

'Anyway,' I said, trying to sit up in my bunk but realising there wasn't enough space between the bed and the ceiling, 'now I don't know what to do. Can I do anything?'

Til sighed. 'Let's review the facts. What do we know? About Shannon. About her dad.'

'Not very much,' I said. 'We know she was in Bodmin

when that photo was uploaded. We know she was carrying a violin. Or a violin case. We also know that her brother thinks she's with their dad. But he also thinks their dad lives in a castle so . . .'

'So he might have had one too many Gummi Bears?'

'Exactly.'

'OK. Right. Well, you've already Googled him, presumably.'

'Her dad? Well.' I paused. 'Not officially.'

'Right,' Til said, in that tone she often uses when she's talking to me – like I'm too stupid to have survived this long.

'Well, what exactly am I supposed to Google?' I protested. '"Shannon's dad, Bodmin"?'

'No, Grace,' Til said patiently. 'You Google his name.'

I paused. 'I don't know it.'

'Jesus, Grace,' Til sighed. I could hear her mum in the background shouting at her. 'I've got to go. But find out the man's name, yeah? That would be a start.'

I lay on my bunk, my head propped up by my rucksack. Til was right. I stood a much better chance of finding a man who *lived* in a town than a girl who was just visiting it. But how to find out his name? The only person I could think to ask was Shannon.

I was in a bit of a chicken-and-egg situation.

What's His Name?

Cool Martin knocked on the door to our room and poked his head round.

'You guys ready for bowling?'

'Yep,' said Ellie.

'Yep,' said Ava.

Ellie dismounted her imagery potter's wheel. Ava grabbed her denim jacket from the hook on the back of the door.

Martin looked up at me where I was still lying on my bunk. 'What about you, Grace? You need a hand getting down from there?'

'I don't know . . .' I said. 'I don't know if I'm going to come, I mean.'

Under normal circumstances, I would've just said I was ill, car sick from the journey or something. But I felt fine, so that wasn't an option. Instead, I kept things vague. 'I think I'm just going to stay here. I want to look at some things on my phone.'

Cool Martin frowned. 'You've come all the way down here just to lie on your bed and look at your phone?'

I nodded. 'It's my favourite thing to do.'

He did a bemused shrug. 'Fair enough.'

When they were all gone, I lay on my back and held my phone above my face. First, I opened Facebook and went to Shannon's profile. I noted there'd been no action or updates since the photo of her at the station. I trawled through her list of friends, scanning the list for anyone with her surname. I'd thought maybe there'd be a relative of some sort, a cousin or an uncle or something, and maybe I could have contacted them, firstly to ask if they'd seen her, or failing that, if they could let me know anything about her dad. His name, for instance. But there was no one. No one with an obvious family connection at all.

This meant the only people I knew, aside from Shannon herself, who could tell me her dad's name were her mum, and possibly Troy. And the problem with this was, I'd got on a minibus and taken myself 240 miles away from them.

I called Til back.

'What's up now?'

'I need a favour,' I said. 'I need you to go back round to Shannon's and ask her mum what her dad's name is.'

'What.'

'Well, I can't, can I? I'm down here now, miles away.'

Til sighed. 'Christ, Gracie. How am I meant to do that? Just rock up and say "What's your ex's name?" She'll never tell me. She'll just get all angry and that. You saw how she was when the kid mentioned the dad that time.'

'She might but . . .' I knew there was a good chance Til was right. 'OK, ask Troy then. Get him on his own.'

'And how am I supposed to do that?'

'I don't know! Take him to the shop. That's what I did.'

Til sighed again – 'Jesus.' – but I knew I'd won her over.

I knew it would take Til some time to get to Shannon's house, to find some way of getting the dad's name out of whoever she found there and then get home again, so I clambered down from my bunk, locked the room door and headed out into the street. I walked up and down for a while, looking in charity shop windows and checking my phone every two minutes. Then I bought an apple juice, sat in a cafe and waited.

When I saw Til's name on my phone screen an hour later, I half expected her to be calling to say she hadn't bothered going to Shannon's house at all. The longer I sat there, thinking about the Clayniacs telling the other teams about the weird girl who'd decided to follow them all the way down there just to sit on her bed, the sillier I felt.

'All right?' Til said.

'Yeah. So did you do it?'

'Well, yeah, I did . . .' She sounded uncertain.

'But?'

'But I'm not sure that Troy kid is all there. Like, I don't know much about kids. Are they all insane or is it just his age?'

Til explained how Shannon's mum had seemed as frosty and worn-out as ever, but that without too much difficulty she'd managed to persuade her to let her take Troy for a kickabout in the park.

'I actually said "kickabout",' Til said. 'Do people really

say that? And then I actually had to kick a ball about with him. It was painful. Why do you make me do these things?'

I ignored her complaints. 'So you asked him his dad's name?'

'Well, yeah. I asked.'

'But he wouldn't tell you?'

'Yeah, he would. He did. It's not that.'

'What is it then? Spit it out, Til! Why are you being so weird?'

She paused. 'The thing was, I couldn't make him talk sense. He said it was . . . Wonder Bingo?'

'Wonder what? Wonder Bingo? That's what he said his dad's name was?'

'Yes.' She sounded sheepish. 'That's what he said.'

'Til! What? That isn't a name. You must have heard wrong. Or he was messing about. You should've made him be sensible!'

'I repeated it back and he just said it again!' she protested. 'He said he was sure. Wonder Bingo.'

'Right.' I sighed. There was no point having a go at Til. I'd seen for myself that Troy just said whatever came into his head. 'OK. Thanks for trying.'

'I asked him again where he lived,' she said.

I perked up. 'Oh yeah?'

'And yeah. He said Cornwall again.'

'Right.'

'In the castle.'

'Great.'

'Maybe it's true,' Til said. 'Maybe their dad's like . . . a clown? Or something. Maybe that's his stage name.'

'OK. Bye, Til.' I put the phone down.

I slumped moodily in my chair, sipping on my apple juice. Then, because the words were in my head rather than because I actually thought I'd find anything, I typed 'Wonder Bingo, Cornwall' into Google.

The results were exactly as I'd expected. Pages and pages of adverts for online gambling sites and bingo halls and arcades in and around Cornwall. All completely useless.

I put my phone face down on the table and drank the last of my drink. I thought about Troy, running along the pavement, his coat flapping behind him like a cape, shouting about castles. He was just a baby. And now this, this 'Wonder Bingo' character. I realised then there was a good chance that somewhere along the line, Troy had confused fiction with reality. Kids did that the whole time. Paddy was forever coming out with stories of how Queen Elsa had helped him put his shoes on at nursery or complaints that Dad wasn't actually Dad but a giant angry swan.

And you could see how it would happen to a kid like Troy. He hasn't seen his dad since he was tiny so he starts believing some film character, or someone from a cartoon or comic, is his dad. Or that's what he wants to believe anyway. This character – Wonder Bingo, living in a castle – was no doubt some superhero or wizard or spy that Troy had got fixated on. It was cute, really. Sad.

I typed 'Wonder Bingo, Castle' into Google and waited to see a page about some adventure film or animated character appear.

When the results came back, there was nothing immediately obvious so I scrolled through the results for a while, until one caught my eye. It was a link to a site of pub and restaurant reviews – dinnerandadrink.com. The preview paragraph under the link said:

. . . Juan-Domingo is the landlord (not Wonder Bingo as I thought he said!) and a great host he is too . . .

Immediately I sat up in my chair. I clicked through to the site. The review was for a pub, and that pub was called:

The Castle.

The Castle Inn, Landwash Nr Bodmin, Cornwall.

I began tapping my phone screen quickly, jumping back and forth between the review site, Google and another web page. It took me less than three minutes to find the website of the Castle Inn in Landwash. And there, on the contact page, was a smiling photo of Juan-Domingo Campos, pub landlord.

I actually laughed out loud.

And then I texted Til:

Juan-Domingo not Wonder Bingo

She replied a few seconds later:

Not my fault the kid's Spanish is rubbish.

Then I stood up, looked around me and wondered how I was going to get to Landwash.

The Castle

A quick map search told me that Landwash was only a couple of miles from where I was in the centre of Bodmin, but it was nearly four o'clock by this point and it was starting to get dark. I knew the Clayniacs would be finished with bowling soon, and I would be expected to meet them to join the other teams for dinner. I didn't really want them to think I'd skipped the entire itinerary just to lie on my bed and look at my phone. And neither did I want to cause Steve any alarm by disappearing off into deepest Cornwall when he was responsible for me.

I went to the counter at the back of the cafe to pay for my juice. The woman on the till was about fifty with long dreadlocks and a strip of fabric tied around her head, like a kamikaze pilot.

'Do you know how I could get to Landwash from here?' I asked as she handed me my receipt. 'Other than walking, I mean.'

She looked at me, blinking slowly like she was just coming out of a trance. 'Landwash? On the bus, my love. Number twelve.'

I pocketed my change. 'Where do I get that from? Do you know where the stop is?'

'You see that hairdresser's over the road?'

I looked to where she was pointing and nodded.

'Just outside, there's a bus stop.'

'Oh yeah. I can see. OK, thanks.' I turned to head for the door, but she put her hand on my arm to stop me.

'Go past that bus stop,' she went on, 'until you get to the butcher's. Then cross the road, and walk towards the statue that looks like a little boy doing a cartwheel. He's meant to be waving a flag but he fell over in a storm and no one's bothered to put him upright again. When you get to the statue, turn around until you're facing the bench and walk forward a few feet and then you'll find a little tiny alley on your left. Go down there – you might have to walk with your hands over your head because sometimes the bushes get quite overgrown – and then you'll come out on another little road. From there, it's just left, right, left again. And you're there.'

I blinked. 'At the bus stop? For the number twelve?'

The woman frowned. 'No. That's where you'll find Linda. She's the lollipop lady for the playschool there. Ask her and she'll point you in the right direction.'

'Right . . . I see . . . I'll . . .' I'd already forgotten three-quarters of what she'd said.

'OK?' she asked, smiling hopefully.

Normally I would have muttered my thanks, made my escape and found someone else, or just tracked down the bus stop on my own.

'Not really.' That was the honest answer. 'I didn't really follow all that.'

The woman sighed and rolled her eyes like she was always having to deal with stupid out-of-towners like me with no idea how to do simple tasks like track down Linda the lollipop lady without someone holding my hand.

She looked at her watch. 'Tell you what, my love, I'm heading that way to catch the bus myself in ten minutes. Take a seat and I'll walk you up there when I've tidied up here.'

I didn't really like the idea of having to make awkward conversation with a chaperone all the way to Landwash but I did need to get there, and if it really was as complicated as the woman had made out, an escort might be necessary.

Ten minutes later, the woman emerged from the kitchen of the cafe wearing a bright pink cagoul and holding a bulging canvas bag in each hand.

'It's good you're coming,' she said, not noticing that she'd knocked two salt shakers and a basket of napkins onto the floor as she bustled past the counter. 'You can help me with that.' She nodded down towards the corner of the room.

I looked down and saw a cage holding a big green lizard. I automatically jumped backwards. 'Argh!'

The woman laughed. 'Don't worry, my dear, it's not real. It's plastic.'

As I peered more closely I could see she was right, although in my defence it was very realistic. But then as I reached out my hand to touch it through the bars, its head turned towards me, it opened its mouth and said, 'So nice of you to drop by!' in a loud New York accent.

I screamed and fell backwards onto the floor from my crouching position.

The woman laughed again. 'Isn't he brilliant? Apparently, it can tell when there's movement nearby and that triggers the voice. Ever so clever. Got it for my grandson. Be a love and pick him up, would you? Can't manage him with all this.' She nodded to her big bags and I did as I was told, struggling to get my arms around the big cage.

The thing about carrying a motion-sensing plastic lizard down a busy high street is that there's a lot of motion for him to sense. This meant that as we walked, the New York lizard chatted almost constantly.

'Look at you!' he called to a man on crutches as I struggled to keep the cage out of his way. 'I like the look of you very much!'

'Well I was *not* expecting this!' he said as a smart businesswoman strode past on her phone.

Things didn't quieten down much when we eventually found the bus stop and boarded the number twelve to Landwash. The lizard was very excited by all the comings and goings down the aisle and everyone getting on or off the bus was treated to an enthusiastic comment. The most excruciating was when a man who looked about a hundred and eight years old slowly made his way up the aisle while the lizard sang him a high-pitched super-fast version of 'I Will Always Love You'.

When we arrived in Landwash, I was pleased to find the cafe woman's ultimate destination – her son's house – was just across the road from the bus stop, so I was able to quickly bid farewell to both her and the talkative lizard, leaving me free to continue my mission in peace.

Landwash was far more the scene I had pictured when I imagined myself in Cornwall. It had a tiny high street – a single short road with a Co-Op, a hairdresser and a post office, and a small patch of green opposite it – a village green.

And across the green was the pub. The Castle Inn.

I made my way over, feeling, for the first time since arriving in Cornwall, a bit nervous.

Despite the cold and the wind and the fading light, there were a couple of old men sitting on wooden tables outside the front of the pub. One of them had a dog at his feet, and I bent down to stroke it, mostly to give me time to think about what I was going to do next. And if I should do anything at all.

I pushed open the heavy wooden door and went inside. There were a few people sitting at tables, reading papers or talking quietly, but it wasn't busy. There was a girl at the bar, drying glasses with a cloth.

She smiled when she saw me. 'What can I get you, darlin'?'

'Uh, well, actually, I'm looking for Juan-Domingo?' I had to admit that out loud it did sound very much like Wonder Bingo. I revised my harsh judgement of Til. And of Troy.

'Juan? He's not here. He doesn't work the bar much any more. Tends to leave it to us.'

'Does he live here though?'

She nodded. 'Yeah. Yeah. When he's home. He's away a lot.'

Another customer came over and ordered a drink and I hovered around, not quite sure where to put myself.

'I was wondering,' I said when the customer had gone. 'Have you seen his daughter? Juan-Domingo's?'

She looked blank, pushing out her bottom lip. 'Daughter? Didn't know he had one.'

I realised then that I hadn't properly considered the idea that Shannon might not be here, in the West Country, at all. Not since finding out about the Castle Inn anyway. It just seemed too much of a coincidence – the photo of her at Bodmin station, Troy thinking she was here, and her dad owning this pub, just a few miles down the road.

'Right,' I said. 'OK.' I looked around the pub. I suddenly wasn't sure what to do with myself. I was stuck hundreds of miles from home on some wild goose chase and the wild goose herself was probably nowhere near here and in no need of my help anyway.

'Can I get you a drink?' the girl said.

'No, thank you,' I said. 'I'm not staying.'

If Shannon wasn't here, there was no point me hanging around in this tiny little village. I turned and headed for the door, wondering how long I'd have to wait before the number twelve would come and pick me up and return me to Bodmin, where at least I had a bed for the night and the prospect of a pizza.

As I walked through the door, I walked straight into one of the old men who had been sitting out the front. He'd been carrying a full pint, three-quarters of which he deposited down the front of my jumper.

'Oh!' he and I shouted at the same time.

'Oh for god's sake,' he grumbled. 'Why can't you kids look where you're going?'

'I did . . .' I started to protest, but before the conversation could go any further, the girl from behind the bar had rushed over.

'Oh, Al,' she said to the man, shaking her head. 'Third time in a week, that is. How do you manage it?'

'It was her!' Al said, sitting down heavily on a bench near the door, complaining loudly about his lost drink.

The girl put her arm around me and ushered me towards the toilets. 'Come here, darlin'. Let me sort you out.'

In the toilets, she dabbed at my front with a thin paper towel but all that did was cover me in tiny balls of wet green tissue.

'Is that better?' she asked anxiously.

I looked down at myself. 'Honestly? No.'

The girl frowned and chewed on her thumb. Then her face brightened. 'I know,' she said. 'Let me get you something dry to wear home. You can bring it back when you've got changed.'

Before I could get into the fact that I didn't plan to be getting the bus back and forth between Bodmin and Landwash the whole weekend, the girl was gone.

I turned on the hand dryer and stood under it, my chest thrust outwards like a gymnast at the end of a routine, in an effort to capture maximum airflow.

A few minutes later the girl bustled back in, her arms loaded with fabric. 'Lost property,' she explained, dropping it on the floor by her feet. 'Stuff people have left behind after one too many.'

She reached down to pick up the item at the top of the pile – an enormous tartan jumper. 'Nice and big, very cosy,' she said, stroking the sleeve and turning it so I could appreciate it from all angles, like she was a presenter on a shopping channel.

I crinkled my nose. 'It looks like it probably smells bad.'

The girl sniffed it, pulled a face and dropped it back on the floor. 'Yes.'

She reached down and picked up a new item. This time it was a pair of plastic dungarees with welly boots built in. 'How about this one then?' She had to stand with her arms right up above her head to demonstrate the full, magnificent length of the piece. 'You could do anything in these!'

I stared at them, trying to imagine what Cool Martin and the rest of the Clayniacs would say if I arrived at dinner in the pizza restaurant wearing a suit surely designed for wading through a sewer.

I sighed. 'No, thank you.' There simply wasn't the time for me to deliver a full honest appraisal of the outfit.

'OK, how about this,' the girl said, undeterred. She held up a white fur coat. 'Lovely and soft.' She rubbed the sleeve against her cheek. 'Like a husky puppy. And smells fresh as a daisy too!' She stepped towards me, holding it up for me to slip on. 'Give it a try,' she said. 'Take that wet jumper off and slide in.'

But I didn't move. I was staring at the coat. 'But that's . . . Shannon's coat . . . ?'

I'd said it more to myself than to the girl. I didn't expect her to have the first idea what I was on about.

'Shannon's?' she said, pulling the coat back towards her and looking at it more closely. 'Oh blimey, I think you're right.' She giggled nervously. 'That was close. Don't know how it ended up in the lost property. Sorry, darlin', that one's off the menu. Cor, she'd kill me if I gave that away.'

She laid it over the radiator and bent down to pick up the next item for my perusal but I stopped her. 'Wait,' I said, pointing at the coat. 'Do you know Shannon? The Shannon whose coat that is?'

The girl looked up, surprised. 'Yeah, course. Juan's lodger. She's been here a week or two, living upstairs.'

'Juan's lodger?'

The girl nodded. 'He's always taking people in. Never any shortage of people looking for a cheap room and Juan'll do anything for a bit of extra cash.'

I didn't have time to go into the ins and outs of how Shannon had come to be in the pub or why or how Juan had invited her to stay. I wanted to find out if it really was her. Although I didn't see how it could possibly be that there was an entirely different Shannon, staying here in this pub, who just so happened to also have a penchant for dressing up like a mountain lion.

'Is she here?' I asked. 'Shannon?'

The girl looked surprised. 'Yeah, probably. Spends the whole time in her room.'

'Can I see her?' I asked. Then I added, 'I think I know her,' in case the girl thought I just wanted to compliment her on her coat directly.

The girl paused for a moment. Then she shrugged. 'I guess so. Out the back, up the stairs, first door on the right.'

All the Way Here

I knocked on the door and waited. It took her a few moments to open it, like perhaps she was contemplating not bothering.

When she saw me, she opened her mouth and closed it again. Then she frowned. 'Grace! What . . . ?'

'Shannon?'

She looked so different. She wasn't wearing any make-up. Instead of her usual skin-tight dress and heels, she was in pyjama bottoms and a big hoody. She looked younger. Smaller, even.

The room behind her was tiny. It had a narrow bed pushed into the corner and a small window, high up and covered by some kind of wire mesh. It looked more like a cell than a bedroom.

'What are you doing here?' she asked.

'I'm . . . I mean, what are *you* doing here? What about the audition?'

At the word audition, it was as if a switch had been flicked, firing the Shannon I knew into action. 'Oh yeah,' she said, tossing her hair back. 'It went really well. Just waiting for a call back. Just chilling out down here in the country while I wait to hear. Because if I get it, things will be non-stop.'

I just looked at her. It just didn't make sense, that she would have an audition, then rather than coming back to her home and college and life, that she would disappear down here, to live in this little cage of a room.

My honest feeling was that she was lying. But then harsh honesty was what had brought me all the way down here to try to make amends. I decided there had to be a middle ground. Honesty, but more gentle. More careful.

'I was worried,' I said. This was true. 'I thought you were upset. I mean, that I had upset you. So I came down here to . . . see.'

Shannon frowned. 'All the way here?'

I nodded.

Shannon didn't say anything. She sat down on her bed, and pulled her sleeves over her hands. 'No one's ever gone to Bodmin for me before. No one's even gone to the shop for me before.'

I didn't say anything.

'Anyway.' She looked up at me. 'Here I am then. You've seen me. Now what?'

It was a good question. I hovered awkwardly in the doorway. I shrugged. 'I guess now . . . now I apologise. For showing you those messages.'

Shannon shrugged. She was staring blankly at the wall in front of her. 'You didn't write them.'

I didn't argue with this. Instead I said, 'I also want you to come back, to Brighton. To college. I feel guilty that you're here, in this little room in this little village because of me. I would feel less guilty if you came back.'

Shannon did a hard laugh. 'Right. Shame about you.'

I sighed and went and sat on the bed next to her. There was a dip in the mattress which meant I sunk in closer to her than I'd planned. 'Your mum's worried about you too, you know.'

Her head snapped round so she was looking at me. 'My mum? What do you mean?'

'She was at college. She asked if I'd seen you.'

'Really?'

I nodded.

Shannon looked confused, like someone had just told her the plot of a film that didn't make sense. 'Weird.'

We didn't say anything again for a while, then I decided to break the silence. 'Look, Shannon, I know there was never an audition. I know that you were upset about the messages and I shouldn't have shown you them, or shown you them in that way anyway, but you've got to come back. You can't just stay here, can you? Your whole life is in Brighton, you can't just walk out of it all of a sudden. What does your dad think? Does he think you should stay or come back?'

Shannon rubbed her forehead with her hand. 'That side of it . . . is kind of complicated.'

Wonder Bingo Himself

Before Shannon could explain what she meant, we heard footsteps on the stairs. Shannon sprung up from her bed and stood in the middle of her room, just as a man appeared in the doorway. He was short and chunky, his polo shirt open at the neck showing a thick silver chain and a little tuft of chest hair.

'All right, Shannon, love?' he said. 'Who's this?' He nodded in my direction. 'Visitor?'

I stood up. 'I'm Grace,' I said. 'Friend of Shannon's.'

The man held out his hand. 'Juan.'

'Juan-Domingo?' I said. I'd been specifically trying to make sure it didn't come out like Wonder Bingo but there really was no way around it.

'Uh, yeah,' he said. 'You heard a lot about me then?' He grinned and folded his arms.

I shook my head. 'Just that you're Shannon's dad, that's all.'

The man frowned and looked at Shannon.

Suddenly, Shannon was wide-eyed. 'I didn't –'

'You what?' the man said to me, his expression somewhere between bemused and scared.

I looked from Juan to Shannon and back again, not sure what I'd said or what was going on.

'I think you've got the wrong end of the stick, love.' He directed the comment at me, but he was still looking hard at Shannon.

No one said anything for a moment.

'I thought you'd recognise me when you saw me,' Shannon said eventually. Her voice was very, very quiet. 'But you didn't. So I thought if I could persuade you to let me stay, it might come to you. If you spent a bit of time around me, you might notice how I walk a bit like you. How I've got your ears. That kind of thing.'

Juan narrowed his eyes and took a step backwards, away from Shannon. 'You said you were travelling. Passing through. You're from London!' He turned away from us for a moment, screwing up his eyes and rubbing them with his fingers like he had a headache.

Shannon didn't say anything.

Then Juan started to laugh. 'I've been had, haven't I? This is a con job. I've heard about these. People turning up pretending to be long-lost relatives. Moving themselves in, bleeding people dry. Is that how it works? You do your research, dig about in some unsuspecting mug's past, work out someone you can pretend to be, then worm your way in and work out a way to cash in?'

Shannon looked like she was going to cry. 'No, I really am –'

'Thing is, though –' Juan went over to the wardrobe, pulled down Shannon's bag from the top, and tossed it on the floor – 'You've messed up this time. Because I don't know where you've got your information from, but there might be a Shannon, and her mother might tell you she's my daughter, but she's never managed to come up with a DNA test. So you're trying to pass yourself off as a daughter I don't even have!'

'I am!' Shannon said, crying now. 'You are my dad! I've seen the birth certificate.'

'You've got fifteen minutes to get out of here,' Juan said. 'Or I'm calling the police.'

He stormed across the landing and into another room. He slammed the door shut behind him.

Shannon sat on her bed and cried. She didn't try to stop it, or even to wipe the tears from her face. I put my arm around her and she buried her face in my shoulder.

'You smell of beer,' she said, her voice muffled with the sobs.

'I know.'

Shannon cried for four and a half minutes (I know because I kept checking my watch, anxious in case Juan was serious about his fifteen-minute calling-the-police deadline) then she stood up, wiped her face on the bottom of her jumper and said, 'What am I going to do, Grace?'

I hesitated for a moment, wondering briefly how it had come to be that I was in the middle of this whole bizarre situation.

Then, calmly and firmly, I said, 'What we're going to do

is this. We're going to pack your bag, we're going to get on a bus to Bodmin and we're going to go out for pizza with some people who really, really like clay. Then tomorrow, we're going to go home.'

Call if You Want

On Sunday evening, after five hours on the minibus listening to Cool Martin telling us how he was robbed to only get second place for the collection of square egg cups he'd managed to expertly fashion during the contest that morning, I went to the Ranch to collect my things from my locker, as instructed by Floyd during my unceremonious telephone sacking.

I'd half thought – hoped – that when I arrived, Floyd might have forgotten all about the phone call, and about giving me the sack at all. Or that perhaps he might be so busy and stressed that he'd just say, 'Oh, you know what, let's forget about that uptight woman. I can't do without you. Just don't overstep the line again, OK?'

But when I got to the Ranch at about eight o'clock, right in the middle of the evening rush, my reception was tense and serious. Teresa took off her sunglasses to give me a sympathetic smile. Dougie rested his massive hand on my shoulder and said, 'We'll miss you, Grace.'

I was overcome with a sudden wave of sadness. It all seemed so final. I liked it there, at the Ranch. I'd just been getting into the swing of things. I knew what I was doing. We all had our little in-jokes. It couldn't really be all over, could it? And aside from that, how would I ever get another job? I hadn't exactly been flooded with offers the first time around.

As I made my way forlornly to the staffroom, opened my locker and begun to drop my things into the empty Tesco bag I'd brought with me for the purpose, I started to feel indignant too. What I'd done had been a *good* thing, if you thought about it properly. It wasn't as if there had been anything in it for me. Quite the contrary. I'd done what I thought was right. Right for Nick. I'd spoken up, put myself on the line, to protect his future happiness. Surely there could be no finer example of putting the customer first? And isn't that what we were supposed to do?

When Floyd rushed past the doorway of the staffroom carrying a tray of empty glasses, I called out after him, 'Floyd! Can I have a word?'

He spun round, his rushed, irritated expression fading as soon as he saw me.

'Ah. Grace,' he said awkwardly. 'I am sorry it's come to this but . . . you did bring it on yourself a bit, didn't you?'

At this point, I had nothing to lose, so I let the full force of my honesty come out, unfiltered.

'Well, actually, no. I don't think I did. On the one hand, yes, I did say some things that *maybe* other people wouldn't have. Maybe other people would have said, "Oh yes, Nick. Proposing to Nikki is a wonderful idea. How romantic!"'

'Yes, they probably would,' Floyd said.

'But would that really have been the right thing to do? Is that really more honourable? I knew that marrying Nikki would have been the worst mistake of Nick's life! Well, OK, I don't know what other mistakes he's made, but I do know that it was not a good idea and wouldn't have made him happy. So all I was doing was thinking of him. I put myself in the firing line, Floyd! I risked getting shouted out by that ice queen – which I did. I risked losing my job just to provide total one hundred per cent customer satisfaction. In fact, in years to come, I expect classrooms of students on hospitality courses will be told about my heartbreaking but inspirational case, as an example of outstanding customer service.'

When I finished my speech, Floyd looked slightly shell-shocked. I folded my arms, head up, defiant. Surely, I thought, he'll see I'm right. He'll apologise, and then he'll offer me my job back.

But what he actually did was start to laugh. 'Oh, Grace,' he said, shaking his head. 'I should've known you'd be a character after that bonkers interview. I can see your logic – sort of – but it's out of my hands. Head Office has spoken. And a word of advice, in your next job, maybe rein in the honesty a bit. Just for self-preservation reasons if nothing else, yeah?'

Then he went back out to the restaurant floor, still shaking his head and laughing and there was nothing for me to do but pick up my Tesco bag of pitiful belongings and leave.

As I made my way out of the restaurant, a few people caught my eye and gave me a wave and or a smile, but most of them were too busy with customers to notice I was going. I couldn't help but feel it wasn't really the type of farewell befitting someone who had sacrificed their career for the happiness of others.

When I was at the door, Floyd called out, 'Oh, Grace, hang on!' He put his tray down on a table and made his way over to me.

Finally, I thought. Better late than never. He's realised I don't deserve this fate.

'I nearly forgot,' he said, reaching into his apron pocket. 'Nick came in. The bloke. He wanted to talk to you but you weren't here. I said you'd call him.'

Floyd handed me a slip of paper and I looked at the handwritten telephone number. I wasn't sure what to make of it.

'He didn't seem angry,' Floyd added. 'I don't think he's going to give you an earful or anything.'

I nodded. 'Right . . . OK.'

'Up to you, anyway,' Floyd said with a shrug. 'Call if you want to. Don't if you don't.'

On my way home, I was sure that I wouldn't call. I was annoyed with him. I knew it was Nikki not Nick who had put in the complaint, but I couldn't imagine he'd stood up to her. I'd put myself out for him and he couldn't be bothered to stand up for me.

But, by the evening, my curiosity had overtaken my irritation. It seemed strange that he should want to speak to me enough to not just pop in on the off-chance of seeing me, but to leave a number with a direct request that we speak. I just couldn't work out what he could want.

What was most likely, I reasoned, was that he wanted to grill me for more details about what I'd said: what exactly had Nikki been doing on her phone? What kind of guys has she been messaging? Did I know any of their names? I had a feeling that Nick would be prepared to go to great lengths to believe it had all been some big misunderstanding.

Still, though, I figured I might as well hear him out.

'It's Grace,' I said when he answered. 'From the Ranch?'

There was a pause for a moment, but then he said, 'Oh hey, Grace!' He didn't sound angry. Or upset for that matter.

'Floyd said you wanted me to call.'

'Yeah that's right, I did . . . listen,' he said. 'I just wanted to say thanks, really. I wasn't . . . I mean, I didn't know how to take it when what happened, happened. When you said what you did and Nikki said what she did and it all got a bit . . . you know. But now a bit of time has passed, I just want to say . . . well, I wanted to say you absolutely saved my life.'

'Oh,' I said, surprised. 'Really?' I knew that was true but I didn't expect him to have realised it quite so soon.

'Yeah! Totally. We had an absolute blazing row after. Even after what had happened, she was still trying to make out that it was all my fault. That I had somehow recruited you as my spy to keep a check on her. She was being crazy. She is crazy.'

'Yeah.' There was nothing else I could say.

'Anyway,' he said. 'I haven't seen her since that night. And good riddance! I'm doing things for me now, not spending all my time and money trying to please her. It never worked anyway.'

'That's great,' I said. Because it was.

'In the last two weeks, I've ridden to Land's End for charity, booked a trip to Amsterdam with my friends and now I'm setting up an adventure centre,' he said. 'It's something I've always wanted to do. Outdoor activities for underprivileged kids – rock-climbing, abseiling, orienteering. I've even got a couple of little boats for sailing lessons – some of these kids have never even seen the sea before if you can believe that! We've already been on the local news and everything, and I've only just started going public with it! Anyway, Grace, I was going to say, if you and your mates want to come and check it out, for a day out or whatever – you can do caving, or maybe go out on one of the dinghies or something. Anything you like. I can sort you out with all the gear. Just to say thanks, you know?'

'Uh, yeah,' I said. 'That's a really kind offer.' I didn't want to have to add 'I can't think of anything worse' but I wondered if honesty required it. But then I had a thought – something else I could say that was equally true but infinitely more useful:

'There is something I'd like actually.'

'Oh yeah?'

'Can we meet to talk about it?'

PART 5:

Where I wonder what actually IS the best policy

No Point Putting It Off

On the Monday morning after our weekend in Bodmin, I sent Shannon a message:

Are you coming to college today?

She replied just as I was leaving the house.

**Going to give it a miss today.
Maybe tomorrow.**

I'd had a feeling this might happen. I thought of Shannon, sitting in her bare bedroom at home, no doubt having had an earful from her mum, nervous of the reaction to her absence from college, and on top of that, still dealing with the beyond-harsh rejection by her dad.

I'd asked her, as gently as I could, on the minibus home if there was any chance she could have been mistaken, and that Juan-Domingo might not be her dad after all. She opened her purse and took out a photo of a small girl sitting on a man's lap in a rowing boat.

'That's me. And him.'

I nodded. I could see she was right on both counts.

'But he never wanted me.' She looked out the window. 'I guess I have to accept that now.'

I messaged her back now:

No point putting it off.
I'll pick you up and we can walk together.

I didn't bother waiting for a reply. Twenty minutes later, I was on her doorstep.

Her mum opened the door. She looked different from the last time I'd seen her. She was wearing jeans instead of joggers, and her hair was loose, not in the tight ponytail.

'You again,' she said when she saw it was me, but with enough of a twitch of her eyebrow and crinkle of her nose to suggest a smile. 'You found her then.'

I nodded.

'I told her that man was a waste of space. I've told her that all along. At least now she's seen it for herself.'

I nodded again, because it didn't seem my place to comment.

Shannon appeared at the top of the stairs. The skyscraper heels were already in place, as was the polar bear coat, which made me smile.

'I don't need a babysitter,' she said crossly as she stomped down the stairs.

'Yes you do,' her mum said.

Shannon just rolled her eyes, picked up her bag and pushed past me out the door. I followed behind.

That morning, we had a Student Team meeting, and to my relief, Ralph and the others didn't make a big thing of Shannon's absence or ask too many questions about her 'audition'. Instead, we picked up where we'd left off last time.

'Grace,' Ralph said, turning to me. 'How are your coconut confessions coming along?'

'Actually,' I said, 'I wanted to talk to you about that. I've kind of been having a bit of a rethink.'

Ralph frowned. 'What kind of rethink?'

I was aware of Shannon sitting to my left. I deliberately didn't look at her.

'I was just thinking . . . maybe they're a kind of lame idea. I mean, it's not like we've all got deep dark secrets. Most of us are pretty boring.'

Ralph said, 'I don't know. I reckon a few people might have something interesting to say.'

I sighed and shrugged. 'It's just a feeling I've been having. Like maybe some things aren't said out loud for a reason. Maybe some things don't need to be said out loud.'

Ralph nodded slowly. 'OK,' he said. 'I can see what you mean. It's your project, after all, this bit. But –' he looked over to the pile of papier mâché coconuts stacked in the corner – 'it seems a shame to waste all that lot. They were starting to look pretty good.'

I looked at the pile. He had a point. They'd taken me ages. 'We can still put them up. We could put something else in them?' I suggested. 'How about . . . sweets? Still do the piñata thing, but just with sweets and toys or whatever.'

Ralph shrugged. 'I guess.'

'Leaves us with another problem though,' Yann piped up. 'What about the Coniston Conscience? I don't think college is going to let us get away with eating sweets as a demonstration of the social's greater good.'

'Good point,' Ralph said.

'I had an idea,' Shannon said. It was the first time she'd spoken during the meeting. We all turned to look at her. 'What if we keep the coconuts as they are, with little messages inside, but just like . . . a different type of message. So instead of confessions we just ask people to write, like, something nice?'

'Something nice?' Ralph asked. 'Like what?'

'Like . . . someone they think is nice or . . . I don't know,' Shannon said quietly. 'Maybe it's a stupid idea.'

'No,' I said, turning to look at her. 'I like it.'

'So it's like, what?' Yann said, looking unimpressed. 'Little love messages like on Valentine's cards? "From your secret admirer" type thing?'

'No,' Shannon said, folding her arms. 'I didn't mean like that. Just forget it.'

'No, I know,' I said. 'I get it. It would be more like, "Grace is really funny and I'm really glad to call her my friend".'

Yann raised his eyebrows.

'Just as an example,' I quickly added.

Ralph nodded thoughtfully. 'OK. Yeah. I see what you mean. It could be kind of sweet, I guess. A bit like . . . radio dedications?'

Shannon nodded and stroked the fur on her coat sleeve. 'Yeah. I guess.'

Ralph looked at his list. 'OK, well do you want to take that on then, Shannon? Swap with Grace and she can do the music?'

'Oh,' Shannon said, looking up. 'I thought I was going to do the music.'

Ralph looked at me, but I didn't say anything.

'What was it you were going to do again?' I said to Shannon, as breezily and innocently as I could manage.

Shannon rolled her eyes. 'Look, would you just trust me, yeah? I know what you think of me, but seriously, trust me. Grace, you can carry on with the coconut thing, you can use my idea. I'm doing the music. Everything just the same as it was before.'

'Shannon,' Ralph started carefully. 'The thing is, the music is a really important part –'

'It's fine,' I said, cutting him off. 'Like she said, everything as it was before. Shannon's on music, I'll sort out the Coconuts of Good. Let's all just . . . focus on our own jobs, yeah?'

Ralph shrugged. 'OK, right you are.'

I Should Iron a Shirt

The following weekend, I went to meet Nick in the place we'd arranged, in the Italian cafe at the marina.

'I must say, I'm curious,' he said as we sat down, him with a teeny tiny coffee, me with a cup of tea. 'What is it I can offer you? I'm afraid a free run up the climbing wall is all I've really got.'

'It's not really for me,' I said.

I took out a piece of paper folded in two from my bag, and passed it to Nick.

He looked at me quizzically as he opened it. 'What's this then?'

I didn't reply at once, I let him scan it.

'Would you give that person a job?' I said. 'If they applied?'

'Applied for what job?'

I shrugged. 'At your adventure centre. For the underprivileged kids. Sailing instructor. Or boat . . . tourer. Something like that. With people. On boats.'

Nick looked surprised, 'Well yeah. I'd give them an interview. We do need someone actually. It's just me and

266

my mate Lee at the moment and he's got his own business to be dealing with.'

'So will you give him an interview?' I said, nodding to the piece of paper.

'I'm confused,' Nick said. 'Whose CV is this? Who are we talking about?'

'My dad.'

Later that evening, I was watching TV with Dad and Ollie when Dad's mobile rang.

'Hello? Yes, speaking. Yes, that's right. Yes, at the marina. I'm just part-time there at the moment though. Sorry, where did you say you were calling from?'

Dad got up and headed out of the room. Ollie looked up briefly, but I kept my eyes firmly on the TV.

Five minutes later, Dad came back.

'Wow,' he said, sitting back down on the sofa. 'That wasn't how I was expecting to end the day.'

'Who was it, love?' Mum said, coming in to join us.

'A guy called Nick,' Dad said, looking up at her. 'He's setting up a new project – a sort of activities and watersports charity for kids who normally wouldn't get the chance. Apparently he's heard about my work at the sailing school and he's asked if I can meet him . . . with a view to offering me a job!'

'What?! Wow, that's amazing!' Mum said. 'And just out of the blue like that!'

'Well, I haven't got it yet,' Dad said. 'But . . .'

'But he's headhunted you, so he must be keen. Who recommended you, did he say?'

Dad frowned and rubbed the back of his neck with his hand. 'He was a bit vague about that. Someone who "knows what a knack I've got with beginners" apparently.'

Mum sat down next to Dad on the sofa and gave his knee a squeeze. He smiled and rested his head on her shoulder.

I took out my phone and sent a message.

Thanks, Nick x

He replied:

No problem. And you definitely don't want me to mention I know you when I meet him?

I thought about this for a moment. It was something that had been on my mind. Was it dishonest to keep Dad in the dark about how Nick had come to hear of his work? And hadn't my indignation at being kept in the dark myself kicked off my whole honesty project in the first place?

I slipped out of the lounge and went upstairs to my room. I looked at my honesty pledge, and the chart below it. Forty-three days crossed off. Seven left. I peeled the chart off the wall and laid it on my bed. I looked at it, lying there.

I heard Mum come up the stairs with a basket of laundry and go into her bedroom to start sorting it into piles.

Downstairs, I heard Dad come out of the lounge and call up the stairs. 'I should iron a shirt. Haven't had to do that for a while!'

Mum came into my room and put a pile of T-shirts and socks on my bed.

She grinned at me. 'Good to see him a bit perkier, isn't it?'

'Yeah,' I smiled back. 'Definitely.'

When Mum had gone to help Dad pick out a shirt, I took my phone out of my pocket and sent Nick a reply:

No. Just don't mention me at all.
Sometimes people don't need to know everything.

Totally Tropical

In order to give people the maximum possible time to get their submissions in, I left the filling of the Coconuts of Good until the afternoon of the social itself.

When I eventually went around the boxes to collect the messages and sat down with them behind the curtain on the stage to review what I had to deal with, I was interested to find that people had embraced this new idea with much more enthusiasm than they had the confessions.

There were still some people determined to make a joke out of the whole thing:

Dear Mrs Lane from the office, your breath is like buttercups. Please will you be my mum?

And some people who had missed the spirit of the exercise:

Niall Palmer, I love how you don't mind that everyone calls you gerbil-face behind your back.

And some messages that were slightly on the creepy side:

Jamie, I sit behind you in art and you don't know my name but I have spent 28 hours and 42 minutes staring at the back of your head and it is beautiful.

But even after filtering these ones out, I still had over fifty nice messages that the students of Coniston College wanted to share with each other. It seemed that, when pushed, everyone was brimming with goodwill for each other. It was really quite touching.

I only had ten coconuts to fill so it took some time to whittle them down, but after two hours tucked away at the back of the stage, surrounded by folded scraps of paper, I finally had ten coconuts, each one filled with a kind message, the hole sealed with a circle of paper stuck down with Sellotape.

With the help of Yann, I hung them all from the cardboard trees already in place around the edge of the hall, ready for eight o'clock, when people would take it in turns to pick up the long wooden stick we used to close the high windows in the art room, and use it to beat down a coconut and read the generous message within. (After discussion with the rest of the Student Team, it had been agreed that, rather than me reading them all out, it was more inclusive if we let the coconut-beater read out the message they had liberated. I was a bit sad to lose my key role in proceedings but I could see their point.)

'I'm seriously worried about the music situation,' Yann

said, as we tied up the last of the coconuts. 'We still don't know anything about it. I don't even know if Shannon's going to turn up.'

I didn't say anything. I had a similar fear but since our Bodmin bonding, I had been very careful not to say anything that suggested I had anything other than complete faith in Shannon's entertainment plan – which was, as far as we knew, still going to centre around her playing a violin. The violin we all doubted she had ever so much as picked up before.

'Well,' I said, 'if the worst comes to the worst, we can just plug one of our phones into the speakers.'

Yann nodded grimly. 'Yeah. Ralph's already put a playlist together.'

Between the end of college that day and the official Totally Tropical social start time of seven o'clock, we all went home to 'get ready'. For me, this meant putting on some deodorant and eating a cheese and tuna sandwich while Paddy sat under the table tucking crayons into my socks.

The Student Team had to be in the hall early, to make sure everything was in place and ready to go. On my way into college, I made a last-minute detour to Shannon's house. I told myself that it would just be nice for us to walk in together, but really I wanted to check she was actually planning on coming.

My worst fears were confirmed when, after several rattles of the letter box, the door went unopened. I pushed open the flap and peered through, but the house was dark and silent. Either Shannon was hiding, or she'd done another runner.

I felt anxious for the rest of the walk to college. Although I knew neither Shannon nor the music arrangements were really anything to do with me, I did feel a certain sense of responsibility. I had spoken up for Shannon, been the only one confident that she wouldn't let us down again. I had a feeling I was going to be made to look like an idiot.

When I arrived at college, I found that I was the first one there. Outside, the barbecue was being set up but inside, the hall was pretty much as I'd left it earlier that day, palm trees and coconuts around the edge, the portable water fountain Yann had managed to borrow from the garden centre trickling away next to the stage, the artificial beach that had taken twenty bags of sandpit sand to create in the corner. But, as well as all this, there were four small boxes positioned across the front of the stage.

I went over to inspect them. They had shiny mahogany shells and a black mesh across the front. I ran my fingers over one.

'Don't stick your fingers through the holes,' a voice said. 'Any damage has to be paid for.'

I looked up. It was a boy I didn't recognise, wearing baggy jeans, a checked shirt and a flat cap.

I stepped away from the box. 'Sorry . . . I –'

The boy laughed. 'I'm just teasing, don't worry.'

Suddenly, Shannon appeared from behind the curtain. 'Karl, you got that ten-metre cable with you? I don't think the six is going to be enough.'

'Shannon!' I said, relieved and surprised to see her.

'Hey, Grace,' she said, too busy trying to break into some

plastic packaging to look up. 'Sorry, can't really stop, we're kind of behind. This is Karl, though.'

Karl reached down from the stage to shake my hand.

'OK . . .' I said. Then, after a pause, 'Sorry, not to be rude but, like, who are –'

'Karl's guitar,' Shannon said, still fiddling the plastic case she was trying to open. 'Or he is today, anyway. Usually he's keys. And John's cello, Martha's vocals. John's got his steel drum with him too, so he can do a bit on that if we want more of a Caribbean feel.'

Two more people stepped out from behind the curtain. A girl a few years older than us, wearing a long skirt and boots, her hair tied up with what looked like a skipping rope, and a man, carrying what I suppose was the cello, but not like any cello I'd ever seen before. It was bright blue, a curl of shiny metal with strings on a black spike down the middle.

'Oh,' I said, taken aback by all these unexpected introductions. 'That's a funny-looking cello. No offence. I just thought they were made of wood.'

The man – John, presumably – laughed. 'It's electric,' he said. 'Hence the amps.' He nodded down at the wooden boxes on the stage.

'Oh. Amps,' I repeated stupidly.

Shannon and the others bustled about, plugging things in, arranging chairs, twanging random strings on their instruments.

'I went to your house,' I said to her. 'To see if you wanted to walk in together.'

'Yeah?' Shannon looked up briefly. 'Sorry. I had to get here early. Soundchecks and that.'

I just watched them for a while, not really sure what to do with myself.

'So,' I said after a while. 'What is it . . . I mean, what are you setting up? Like, what's going to happen?'

Shannon gave me a funny look. 'I'm setting up for the gig, Grace. Like we talked about a million times.'

'Right,' I said slowly. 'So this is . . . a band.'

'Yes, Grace,' Shannon said with a sigh. '*My* band.'

'So you're going to . . . do something, in it?'

'Yes, Grace,' Shannon said again. 'I'm going to play the violin. Here it is, see?' She flicked open a black case and took out an instrument. Again, it was nothing like the brown wooden violins I was used to. It was bright white with a black neck. 'It's electric too, before you ask. Sometimes we do traditional stuff but we thought as it's a party, we'd do something a bit more modern. That OK with you?'

I nodded. 'Yeah. Course. OK.'

Even then, I still couldn't imagine it was true. That Shannon really would be about to play a difficult instrument like the violin to a standard good enough to make it an appropriate soundtrack for a party.

I was distracted from the band by the arrival of Ralph, closely followed by Yann and Beth, all of whom exchanged subtle surprised looks at the sight of Shannon amongst all these instruments, but all of whom decided not to comment. Instead, we left her to her preparations and busied about for twenty minutes, closing blinds, stringing up fairy lights and stacking cupcakes on an enormous tiered stand shaped like a pirate ship.

'Ralph, Karl's just going to do some quieter stuff on the guitar while we wait for everyone to arrive, then we'll do the full set from about half seven, yeah?'

'Oh,' I piped up. 'What about the –'

'Don't worry,' Shannon said with an indulgent smile and slight eye-roll. 'We'll take a break at eight or whenever you want to do the coconut smashing.'

'Yes,' I said. 'Right. Good.'

Just before seven, Karl and his guitar took to the stage and I was relieved to see that he at least knew what he was doing with a stringed instrument. It was all very beautiful and folky and I personally would have been quite happy to let him go on all night. But, as promised, just after half past seven, the whole rest of the band emerged from backstage to join him. As Shannon straightened her dress then put her violin under her chin, Ralph and I exchanged a look, a raised eyebrow each as if to say, 'Here goes then.'

But here's the thing: they were amazing.

Shannon was actually amazing.

I don't know exactly how good you have to be at violin to be 'basically grade eight standard' but I don't think I could have been more impressed if she had set the thing on fire and played it blindfolded. The whole band were brilliant. Just as good as anything you hear on the radio and I don't just mean the terrible crackly old music programmes Mum and Dad listen to on a Sunday morning. This was proper professional pop music.

'Well, I didn't see that coming,' Til said, appearing next to me and handing me a drink.

I shrugged. 'I guess she doesn't lie about everything.'

'Maybe she *is* the hundred-metre world record holder after all . . .' Til said.

I just smiled.

Reeta was sitting on the deck chairs that had been set out along the fake beach and Til and I went to join her. We weren't talking for a moment, just sitting, sipping our drinks and listening to the music when Sarah walked past, right in front of us. I felt myself sit up straight. I hadn't even known she'd be coming. I assumed she'd be off, doing something cooler, with her cool, out-of-college mates. I assumed she'd have no interest in coming to something I'd organised.

She looked at me, and our eyes met, just for a second. I attempted a smile, but she looked away before I'd really got into it. Then she walked quickly across the hall towards the drinks table. She didn't look back.

'Oof,' Til said. 'What was that about? She properly blanked you.'

I didn't say anything. I could feel my cheeks burning. I suddenly thought I might cry.

'Oh, Christ,' Til said, chewing on her lip. 'Don't blub.'

I scowled. 'I'm not.'

'What happened?' Til said.

So I told her about my conversation with Sarah on the pier, and my completely honest assessment of her and our relationship.

277

Til just stared at me. 'You called her boring?'

'What?' I said crossly, pushing my hands into the pockets of my hoody. 'I said *sometimes* she was boring. And sometimes *I* was boring! I was just being honest.'

Til closed her eyes briefly for a second, like a mother who had just discovered her child had drawn all over the wall with permanent marker. Then she opened them and said, 'Do you think, Gracie, that there are times when one hundred per cent, smack-me-in-the-face total honesty isn't the absolute best policy?'

I scowled some more. And then I said. 'Yes, actually, I had started to consider that.'

Til just sighed and shook her head. 'Oh, Grace.'

We were quiet again. Reeta was eating her way through a plate of cupcakes, pink icing somehow getting up her nose and in her eyebrows.

'But what I just can't work out,' I said after a while, 'is if it's not lying and it's not honesty, then what actually *is* the best policy?'

Til shrugged. 'I don't know, man. Whatever's *best* is the best policy. Sometimes it's too complicated to make a rule.'

And That is the Honest Truth

As promised, just before eight, the band stopped at the end of their song, and Martha the singer said, 'OK, guys, we're just going to take a short break now because I understand you're doing some kind of event.'

She looked over expectantly towards Ralph and me, for someone to take over the hosting of proceedings.

I looked at Ralph. He looked at me. 'It's your thing,' he said with a shrug. 'Want to do a little introduction or something?'

I paused. 'I don't know,' I said. 'Being the centre of attention both excites and dismays me.'

Ralph grinned and gave me a little shove. 'Just get on with it'.

I stepped up onto the stage and stood in front of the microphone. There were three bright lights on the ceiling shining right in my face, so I couldn't really see who I was talking to.

'Uh, hi,' I said. 'So we're going to do a thing now, that was sort of my idea and sort of Shannon's idea . . . sort of two ideas, mixed together . . . and what it is, is that, you know, or you probably know, that I've been asking you ask to submit little nice messages, little . . . nuggets of warmth and affection. Well, I've collected these up and put ten of them in the coconuts you can see around you. And in a minute, we're going to hit them down with a stick and read out the messages.' I paused. 'And I know it sounds random, but I think it's a really good idea of Shannon's – because the nice bit was Shannon's idea – because before we were going to have confessions but some people got a bit . . . carried away, and I think it's much nicer if we're . . . well, nice. So . . .'

'Get on with it,' Til called from the audience. It was exactly typical of me to get heckled by my best friend.

I breathed out. 'OK, yes. Fine. Anyway, you should all have been given a raffle ticket on the way in. I've got the matching numbers here.' I picked up the bowl of tickets from the back of the stage. 'So, if your number's called, step forward and . . . unleash the love!'

Luckily everyone seemed in high spirits and started clapping and cheering, so I didn't have to dwell on how or why I had just said 'unleash the love' out loud to a room full of people.

The first ticket out of the bowl was number eighty-five and belonged to a girl called Mary who beat down the first coconut as if that was what she had been born to do. When it fell to the floor, she stepped forward and picked up the tiny scroll of paper. The room fell silent in excitement and anticipation of what the message would say.

'It says,' she said in a clear voice: '"I hated my old school and every day I would dread going in. Since joining Coniston I have real friends for the first time. I love it here."'

There were a few 'ah's from the room and someone called, 'Who's it from?'

'No names,' I said into the microphone. 'It's all anonymous.'

'There's a bit more,' Mary said. Then she carried on reading. '"Especially thanks to K, P, J and L."'

From the group hugging going on in the corner between Kirsty, Paige, Jasmine and Lara, with Maddie Wise very much in the middle, I think we could be fairly certain who submitted that one. Still, it didn't matter. Everyone was getting into the spirit of the activity nicely.

We repeated the procedure for the next eight coconuts and as each one was smashed and each message read out, I felt rather pleased with myself. Of course, the messages had come from other people, but I think I'd curated the selection expertly.

There were messages of general thanks and love to the college as a whole, from people who generally felt that life was better since they'd started there.

There were some more targeted messages, for example, someone wanting everyone to know how Connor Smith had spent so much time tutoring them in maths that they had finally passed their Maths GCSE 'on the fourth attempt, and the only sad thing is I won't get to see Connor so much any more'.

Coconut number six was a message to Mrs Brookes the college librarian who was retiring next term, and who 'was so much more than a librarian. You've been my counsellor, my cheerleader and my friend'.

Mrs Brookes started to get a bit teary at that point, and when I decided it was only fair to step forward to the mic to let the room know that that message was actually one of nine or ten about her, lots of other people lost it too and we had to have a five-minute tissue break.

To stop it all getting a bit too much, I'd also included some more light-hearted ones, like the message that might have worked just as well for the honesty coconuts, from someone keen to tell 'GV' that they really liked her pineapple-print jacket: 'in fact, I like it so much that it's currently in my own wardrobe for safe-keeping'.

Coconut number ten was the one I was really interested in though. As I reached in to choose the number of the person who would be asked to crack it, I silently hoped it would be someone good. If the message was read out by someone who couldn't quite read properly or who had a voice like a chipmunk, it was going to take the edge off things a bit.

'Number forty-two!' I called.

'Yep! That's me!'

I looked up. It was Cool Martin. I smiled to myself. He was up to the job, I reckoned.

Cool Martin very coolly swiped the coconut down with one stroke, slid it down the pole to his hand, and cracked it open on the wall next to him. He took out the message and carefully uncurled it.

'This is a message for S,' he read. '"Just to say, she is very patient and kind and nicer than a lot of people, especially people who call her boring. And for the record, she is actually the opposite of boring. And that is the honest truth."' Martin looked around, grinning. 'So, well done, S!' Then he added, 'That bit was just from me. It doesn't actually say "well done" on the paper.'

'Yes, great, thanks, Martin,' I said into the mic before he could freestyle any more and ruin the tone of the message. 'Anyway . . . that's the end of coconut messages . . . so I'll hand things back to the band!'

I don't know if the cheering and whooping that followed was for the band or for the Coconuts of Good or just a sign of the general party mood, but as I walked off the stage to Martha singing the first few lines of 'With a Little Help from My Friends', it seemed the Totally Tropical social was proving to be a success.

I got myself a new drink from the table and headed outside to get some air and see if any of the barbecue food was ready yet. I looked around for any sign of Til and Reeta, but couldn't see them. Knowing how much Til hated emotional scenes I half-wondered if she'd walked out during the Mrs Brookes sob-fest.

I leant against the wall and took a sip of my drink.

'That was really nice.'

I looked up. Sarah was standing in front of me.

'Oh, hi,' I said, quickly wiping my face with my sleeve and hoping I didn't have a cherryade moustache.

She came to lean on the wall next to me.

'It was nice,' she said again. 'The whole coconut thing. It was a nice idea.'

I shrugged. 'It was Shannon's idea really.'

'She grown on you then, has she?' Sarah nodded through the window towards the stage, where Shannon was in the middle of a scarily good violin solo, her bow swooping back and forth, her hair swishing from side to side.

'Yeah,' I said. 'I guess she has.'

We didn't say anything for a moment. We both took a sip of our drinks.

'That last message . . .' Sarah said. 'It was . . . nice. Whoever it was about. Whoever it was from.'

I smiled shyly. 'Maybe there are lots of S-people at college. And maybe lots of people who think they're the opposite of boring.'

Sarah smiled and took my hand in hers. We stayed like that for a minute, holding hands, leaning against the wall, looking up at the sky.

Then she said, 'You know, Grace, even though we've got nothing in common, even though we don't always get each other, I still think you're pretty special. I hope we can be friends. Proper friends.'

I gave her hand a squeeze. 'I hope so too.'

Read on to see what Gracie
gets up to next, in
By Popular Demand

PART 1:

Where I contemplate a future with only a pie for company

Hoe-down

It was Saturday night and I was having a perfectly sophisticated evening in with my two good friends, Til and Reeta. We were in my bedroom watching a critically acclaimed French film set in picturesque Provence. I had laid on an elegant buffet of culinary delights, inspired by cuisines from around the world.

'Why is it all so small?' Til said, picking up a bite-size feta-and-tomato tart. 'It makes me feel like a giant, holding this fiddly little stuff in my big hands.'

'That's how it's supposed to be,' I explained. 'They're appetizers. *Hors d'oeuvres.*'

Til looked at me, then down at the snacks, then at me again. Her face was blank.

I sighed. 'It's not meant to be *dinner*. I never said I was making you dinner. They're just to taste. They're *amuse-bouches*. They're meant to *amuse* your *bouche*.'

Til frowned, pushed the tiny tart into her mouth and chewed thoughtfully.

'Why have you put the grapes on sticks though?' Reeta

asked, picking up a cocktail stick and twirling it around.

'They're not grapes,' I told her. 'They're olives.'

Reeta put one in her mouth, but after just one chew her eyes widened and she spat it back into her hand. 'I think they're off, Gracie,' she said, wiping her mouth with the back of her hand.

'They're not off, I only got them today.' I put one in my mouth. 'See,' I said, chewing the salty ball. 'They're fine. They're . . . delicious.' I forced myself to swallow.

Reeta tipped the mangled remains of hers into a plant pot in the corner of my room. 'Sorry,' she said, shaking her head sadly. 'I think my tongue is allergic to them.' She reached into her bag and took out a pint-size carton of milk and drank it down in one go.

'They're just an acquired taste,' I said, taking another olive from the plate. 'If you don't get through the barrier, you'll never acquire it.'

Til frowned. 'As in, no pain, no gain?'

I nodded. 'Exactly. We're in college now, for heaven's sake. We need to make an effort to mature. Do you want to be the only adults in history to still be eating Cheestrings and boxes of raisins like a baby? Because I do not.'

Til peered at the olives again, but decided against taking one. She leant against the end of my bed and turned back to the television.

Although the film was very interesting and packed full of beautiful fields of wild flowers and farmers having lively conversations in the middle of those fields, I was checking my phone regularly. Every thirty seconds, to be precise.

This wasn't because I was bored, you understand, but just in case some very serious news should break that I would need to report to the others.

As I scrolled through with one eye on the TV, where a French farmer was shouting angrily at the sky, I noticed that a lot of the photos in my feed seemed to have been taken in the same place: some kind of American diner. It had a bar lined with neon-pink lights and posters from classic films all over the walls.

Lots of the photos showed people from college standing behind the bar, spooning ice cream into blenders or stirring big glasses with stripy straws. Everyone seemed to be wearing strange clothes. Ellie from my business studies class was wearing what looked like a cheerleader's dress, with a set of poms-poms slung over her shoulder. Jonathan Jones – or Jon-Jon as everyone called him – was dressed as a cowboy, and Martin had, for some reason, wrapped himself in a sheet, put on a spiky cardboard hat and painted his face grey.

'Is *everyone* from college in a diner tonight or what?' I passed my phone to Til and she squinted at the screen. 'And what are they all wearing? "American Dream", they're all saying. "Hashtag American Dream". What are they *doing*?'

'It's for Jon-Jon's birthday,' Til said, passing my phone back to me. 'It's an American party in that new diner by the pier.'

New photos were appearing every few minutes or so. In the latest batch, Martin seemed to be holding his sheet-skirts up around his knees and tap dancing. 'Why has Martin come as a Roman?'

Till shrugged. 'They're doing a milkshake workshop first. Then later there's going to be music and that. Jon-Jon's got the whole place hired until eleven. Should be a cool night.'

I sighed. 'Why do *we* never get invited? Why do we never get invited to cool nights?'

Til didn't reply, which wasn't unusual, but Reeta was staring hard at the television, her mouth clamped shut like she was afraid some words might escape if she didn't very consciously hold them in. She wasn't even blinking.

'Reeta . . . ?'

'Nope!' she said, in a too-loud voice, her eyes still fixed on the screen. 'No! Nothing!'

I frowned. 'What's nothing?'

She looked at me then, her eyes wide. 'I don't know! Nothing!'

I peered at her. 'You were invited, weren't you? To Jon-Jon's American hoe-down milk-fest diner-thon?'

Reeta still didn't say anything. She just turned to look at Til, who shifted uncomfortably on her bean-bag.

'You as well!' I threw an olive at her.

Til ducked and the olive bounced off the window sill and into my laundry bin. 'Sorry, man. But, I thought you didn't like Jon-Jon? Remember, you said he always talks like a gameshow host?'

'He does! Everyone says that!'

'Yeah, but you said it *to* him.'

I was quiet. He did talk like that. He would put his arm around your shoulder and lean in far too close and say, "Hello, Grace, and how are you today, are you having a good day?" And then if you ever tried to reply to him he would get bored immediately and start talking over the top of you. Til was right. I didn't like him. But that was hardly the point.

'That's hardly the point,' I said. 'Loads of people don't like him. You don't like him. But you're invited and I'm not. It's . . . victimisation!'

Til rolled her eyes. 'We're here, aren't we? We're here now, at your French film and amusing-bouche evening, rather than down at the diner?'

'I was just thinking actually . . .' Reeta began quietly and I turned to look at her. She picked up a magazine, rolled it into the shape of a tube, angled it in Til's direction and spoke into it, as if that way I wouldn't hear what she was saying. 'We should . . . go . . . ?'

She looked at Til nervously.

Til frowned. 'Reeta!' she hissed.

I looked between them. 'What? What's this? Where should you go?'

They looked sheepishly at each other, and then down at the ground.

'Oh, right. I get it.' I folded my arms. 'I see what's going on here. You're going, aren't you? That's your real plan for tonight. You just popped in here to keep me quiet – to do your bit and entertain your loser friend for a few hours – but you both can't wait to get out of here and down to the proper party!'

Neither of them said anything.

'Fine,' I said, turning off the TV and tossing the remote

down on the duvet. 'Go. Go on. Go and wrap yourself in a sheet and eat hot dogs made of horse's hooves and wave your stars-and-stripes flags. It's quite clear my efforts at real food and sophisticated entertainment are wasted on you.'

'We do need to get going . . .' Til said quietly.

They both got to their feet and picked up their stuff.

'Sorry, Gracie,' Reeta said, taking her coat down from the hook on the back of my bedroom door. 'Thanks for –'

'Just go!' I said, cutting her off and turning my head away from them as they made their sorry exit.

Once they'd gone, I prepared myself a small platter of olives, feta tarts and slices of expensive cooked ham. I put the film back on and tried to concentrate on the subtitles as one man in a hat told a man in a different type of hat something very important about the ground.

Obviously, I'd much rather be here, I told myself, with this intelligent film and this elegant finger food. Far better to be indoors, in my own space, enjoying the peace and quiet, than wearing some ridiculous outfit in a sweaty diner with boring idiots like Jon-Jon talking over everyone.

I couldn't stop myself from taking a few sneaky looks at my phone though and it wasn't long before, in the constant stream of photos everyone seemed to feel the need to upload, Til and Reeta appeared. Til was wearing a yellow T-shirt with 'lifeguard' written across the front in big red letters and was carrying a red plastic swimming float. Reeta had handcuffs dangling from one wrist and was wearing a bright orange jumpsuit like a prisoner would wear.

I didn't see what any of it had to do with America. There were lifeguards and prisoners in all countries, weren't there? Really, what was the point in having a theme if no one was even going to stick to it?

My phone flashed. A video upload from Martin. It was of himself, grinning at the camera in his strange sheet costume, holding a cone of chips.

I typed a reply.

Me: Why are you dressed as a Roman emperor?

Martin: Statue of Liberty! Why aren't you here?

Me: Not invited

Martin: Sucks to be you!

I turned the TV off again and shoved the remote under my pillow.

Martin was right. It did.

Sheila Wheeler

I'd started my new job at Podrick's Hardware Store just a few weeks earlier.

It was little shop down a quiet road on the way to Til's flat that had probably been the same for about a hundred years and sold everything from sink plugs and hammers to yoga bricks and fairy lights shaped like flamingos. When I'd been unceremoniously sacked from my last job at a steakhouse called the Ranch, my only crime being to offer a regular customer my services as a love-life advisor, I thought I might never work in this town again. But luckily I'd only been unemployed for a few days when Leonard, the owner of Podrick's, agreed to take me on.

The shop was tucked away so it was usually quite quiet and I spent most of my shifts there flicking through a magazine or looking at my phone behind the till, occasionally looking up to ring through a bottle of carpet shampoo or a mousetrap. Once or twice a week a customer would hugely overestimate my knowledge of the products in the shop and how they should be used, and would ask me what kind of fixture they should buy to put up a mirror or what size batteries they needed for a portable disco ball. If I was feeling helpful when they asked, I would look up the answer on my phone but, more often than not, I'd direct them to my colleague, Sheila Wheeler, who had worked at Podrick's for years and years.

Sheila Wheeler may have been eighty years old or may have been forty. There was really no way to know for sure. She had white hair that stuck straight out of her head like a candy-floss hat; she wore a watch around her neck on a chain and kept a cigarette tucked behind her ear at all times. Sheila could tell you not only exactly which product was stored in which section of which shelf in the shop, but she could tell you what used to be shelved there on any given year in the past and exactly when and why it had been replaced. There wasn't a square foot of the shop that Sheila didn't know the entire history of.

'Do you know where the de-icer's kept?' I'd ask, for example.

'Far-left corner, third shelf from the bottom, two blocks in.' But she wouldn't stop there. 'Just above the fingerless gloves. Where we used to keep the candles from 2004 to 2006 and where we used to keep the light-up yo-yos until that little lad swallowed a bulb and the whole lot had to be sent back to the factory.'

I didn't mind Sheila. After my first hour in the shop, she treated me as if I'd worked there my whole life. This did mean that she seemed surprised when I didn't know how to change a till roll or when I didn't realise that the blue neon sign reading FIRE that flashed from time to time just meant that there was a delivery at the back door and not that we needed to evacuate immediately, but it also meant she left me alone. She would tuck herself away in the corner of the shop, sometimes tidying shelves and restacking tea towels, sometimes just doing the crossword on the back of the paper, and I was free to sit behind the counter and mind my own business.

The day after Jon-Jon's American Dream milkshake party that I wasn't invited to, I had a shift at Podrick's starting as usual at 9 a.m. I was still grumpy about being left out and had ignored three messages from Reeta and one from Til.

A man in bright-red trousers and a waistcoat strolled into the shop. He wandered around with his hands in his pockets, whistling like he'd come for a day out rather than to buy anything in particular. He stopped in front of the Bargain Bucket – a wire basket we kept just in front of the till, labelled with a sign saying:

All items £1

'Everything one pound, is it?' he said.

'Yes, that's right,' I said. Then I added, 'Just a pound,' because it felt like I should say more, but there really wasn't anything else to say about it.

He picked up a bottle opener shaped like a garden spade. 'A pound?' he asked.

'Yep,' I said.

'And this?' This time he was holding up a packet of gold pens.

'One pound, yes. Everything in there is a pound.'

He nodded and continued to rifle through. Then a smile crept slowly over his face. 'How about,' he said, holding up a can of air freshener in one hand and a packet of radish seeds in the other, 'if I want two things? Bet it's not one pound then, is it?'

I frowned at him. 'That would be two pounds,' I said slowly. 'One pound for each item.'

'Aha!' He threw the things back into the basket. 'I knew it! There is always a trick with these things! That, young lady, is why I always read the small print.'

'OK,' I said, because really, what else was there to say?

With this, he clearly felt his point was made and his use for the shop was exhausted because he strolled out, shaking his head and muttering, 'One pound, my foot.'

When he'd gone, Sheila ambled over to the counter. She unfolded the fraying deck-chair she kept tucked underneath it and sat down heavily. She placed her crossword in her lap and took a pencil out of the pocket of her Podrick's T-shirt.

'He was a plonker, then,' she said, nodding her head in the direction of the door the man had just left through. 'Some people talk to strangers just to hear the sound of their own voice, don't they.'

'Yeah.'

'I myself can't bear it,' she went on, leaning over her crossword with her pencil poised. 'My old dad – dead and gone now, died in '98 – he used to say to us kids that when we're born we only have a certain number of words in us to last a lifetime and that when they were used up, that was it.

So we shouldn't prattle on too much because we might find when we're thirty-five we've run out all together and we can never say another word.' She paused while she carefully filled in some of the boxes in her puzzle. 'It worked, I can tell you. We weren't talkers, any of us in our house. We could go a whole weekend and the only words that would break the silence would be "pass the fruitcake" and "has anyone seen my underpants".'

My phone vibrated on the top of the counter. It was another message from Til. I didn't bother opening it.

'I don't know how you bear it,' Sheila said, nodding towards the phone. 'Dreadful things. I would never have one. I haven't even got one in my house, let alone one you have to cart about with you.'

'You haven't even got a house phone?'

She shook her head. 'Nope. Got rid of it in 2005. Had enough of people ringing up, trying to sell me things, night and day.'

'What about if someone wants to talk to you? How do you arrange stuff? What if you want to meet someone? How would you know where to go?'

Sheila laughed loudly like I'd made a great joke. 'Meet who! Why would I want to meet anyone? When I go home from this place of an evening, I close the door and I know I'm not going to see another living person until I come back here. I feel sorry for people whose lives are filled with having to meet people, one after another. Always someone's wedding or tea party or birthday to go to.

'I tell you, for my birthday last year I got one of the

good pork pies from Waitrose and a bottle of nice ale and I sat down in front my own telly and I watched the entire final of the 1992 American Open. Sampras and Edberg. An absolute corker of a match. I watch it every year, for my birthday. Just me, the pie, the tennis. No people turning up with their cheap flimsy cards to clutter up the shelves. No dried-up pot plant or itchy pyjamas I have to pretend to like. No sitting around listening to people whinge about their children or their grandchildren or why the gear stick's wobbly on their Ford Focus. Just me, on my tod. And a very happy birthday it was too.

'Because that, I tell you, Grace my girl, is the route to true happiness. Ditch the hangers-on. I can see you're like me at heart, you haven't got time for it all either. It's tough, I know, when you're a young thing like you are, to be true to yourself. I know there's pressure to be on the phone, to be talking talking talking on the bus, hanging around in a gaggle like noisy geese, invited to parties every night . . .'

'Actually, I don't get invited to parties,' I said bitterly.

'Well, good!' Sheila pointed her pencil at me triumphantly. 'Good for you. You're well on your way. By the time you're twenty, you'll be partying like I do. Just you and a pork pie. Because people like you and me have worked out your own company is best.'

With this final proclamation, Sheila turned her attention back to her puzzle. She carefully wrote the word CACTUS as the solution to 9 down.

When my shift was over, I took my phone out of my bag and rang Til before I was even at the end of the road.

'Til,' I said as soon as she answered. 'I need more friends. Immediately. Please do not ever let it happen that my only friend is a pork pie.'

It had occurred to me with increasing panic that even my three-year-old brother Paddy, whose best friend was a stuffed Lizard called Dustbin, had a livelier social life than I did, being invited as he was to parties most weekends.

Til yawned. 'You what? Are you still sulking about the America party? It was only OK, you know. Average. It wasn't the best night ever or anything.'

'Well, that's great, isn't it! I can't even get invited to the average nights!'

'You don't like Jon-Jon,' Til said. 'And actually, didn't you say that an American diner was the last place you'd want to hang out and that you'd seen enough milkshakes and grilled meat to last a lifetime when you worked at the Ranch?'

'But Til, that's not the point! Not liking things is my choice. Being left out of things is not!'

Til paused. 'So just to confirm my understanding is correct: you feel left out of things you don't want to do, by people you don't even like?'

'Exactly.'

Til sighed. 'Right. So, what are you going to do about it?'

'I'm going to change things! I'm going to get popular!'

Jess Vallance

Jess Vallance works as a freelance writer and lives near Brighton. Her YA novels for Hot Key Books are *Birdy* and *The Yellow Room*, as well as the first Gracie Dart novel, *You Only Live Once*.

Follow Jess at www.jessvallance.com or on Twitter: @ JessVallance1

HOT
KEY
BOOKS

Thank you for choosing a Hot Key book.

If you want to know more about our authors
and what we publish, you can find us online.

You can start at our website

www.hotkeybooks.com

And you can also find us on:

We hope to see you soon!